Sumatra Alley

Sumatra
Alley

❋❋❋❋❋❋❋❋❋❋❋❋❋❋❋❋❋❋❋

by

MERLE CONSTINER

THOMAS NELSON INC.

New York   Camden

All rights reserved under International and Pan-American Conventions. Published in Camden, New Jersey, by Thomas Nelson Inc. and simultaneously in Don Mills, Ontario, by Thomas Nelson & Sons (Canada) Limited.

First edition
ISBN: 0-8407-6126-0
Library of Congress Catalog Card Number: 79-140080
Manufactured in the United States of America

To Susannah

Sumatra Alley

1

In the southern part of New York City in
1765, not far from the waterfront, was a narrow, crooked,
cobblestoned street known as Sumatra Alley. It got its
name from the forest of shipping that clogged its mouth
at Coenties Slip, the giant Indiamen perpetually berthed
there, with the ghosts of Java, Canton, Sumatra, and
Borneo in their salt-stained canvas. Once it had been
the spice district, but as the port mushroomed in its
growth and the neighborhood became compressed, the
spicemills scattered and moved elsewhere in the city.
Now it was a cluster of small workshops and kitchen-
factories for the crafts and trades; and not only for the
crafts and trades, but for the most highly skilled of the
crafts and trades.

Two goldbeaters were here, and a deluxe confectioner, a midget waxworks where scientific models for
medical study and demonstration were constructed, and
a half dozen other establishments, including a print-
shop and a maker of harpsichords.

In the whole teeming city, and Brad Agnew knew it
all, from its most fashionable tree-lined avenue with
its imposing mansion facades to its most squalid back-
streets and dingy cul-de-sacs, Sumatra Alley, outwardly
serene and quiet, seemed the very last place a man
would expect big trouble.

Brad Agnew was seventeen years old, stocky and soft-spoken, with his sandy hair always in a neat tight queue overlapping the back of his threadbare collar. His father had been killed by the Indians up in the north country, almost at the cabin doorstep, when Brad was two, and he couldn't remember him at all, hard as he sometimes tried. His mother had brought him down to New York City then, right away, and right away, too, she'd caught the fever and died. So he couldn't really remember her, either. It had been the House of Refuge for him then, the Almshouse, and afterward three or four years when he had grown up with the expanding port, mainly on its streets. He had wanted to be a doctor, even then.

He was thirteen years old when Dr. Doddridge had seen him putting a makeshift splint on a dog's leg by the public pump, had talked to him, and had brought him here, to his shop and home.

That was the way it had happened. Just like that, almost as quick as you could snap your fingers, he'd had a second father, a real-live one it seemed this time, and a real home.

Dr. Doddridge, once a famous surgeon in London, had been middle-aged when he came to America. He was elderly now, and rarely practiced anymore. He was obsessed by two things—instructing Brad in the fundamentals of medicine and surgery, and working on his anatomical wax models. It was the sale of these models, created jointly now by Brad and the doctor, that gave them their meager livelihood. There was a time when Brad could not have imagined he could ever be so happy.

The neighbors of crooked, cobblestoned little Sumatra

Alley were like members of a family. And like members of all families, some were—well—a little more pleasant than others, to put it mildly. But that was natural.

It was eleven o'clock at night and Dr. Doddridge had gone to bed. Had just gone to bed, as a matter of fact, for the people of Sumatra Alley, who worked with their brains and hands, served under the cruelest of all taskmasters, themselves.

Brad put a cagelike muslin dust shield over the replica he had been working on—a flexed arm in four layers, skin, muscle, veins, and bone, beautifully done in wax, exquisitely tinted in blue and carmine, lavender, and chalk-white—and carefully cleaned and put up his modeling tools. As he banked the workfire in the big fireplace and gathered up the day's wax remnants and stowed them in the cupboard, he saw that his hand trembled a little, from the ordeal of concentration he had just passed through. He decided a little chat with Piggot might relax him before he went to bed.

Piggot was helper and bondboy to Duquesne, the master confectioner, and Brad's closest friend.

He went up the steep chimney stairs, past his bedroom door at the landing, up the ladder, and through the trapdoor to the roof.

The sky was a deep blue, with a swirl of stars like powdered glass. No sound or tint of light came up from the chasm of the street at his left. Before him, at different levels, but only at slightly different levels, were the flat roofs of the continuous row of shops, some with patchwork squab hatcheries, each with its tangled clotheslines and solitary indistinct chimney and chim-

ney pot. This was an almost nightly journey for Brad.
Duquesne's was three chimneys down.

The eaveline here was broken by the ridge of a dormer
window, Piggot's attic bedroom window. The window
showed light; Piggot was still awake. Brad lifted the
Duquesne rooftrap, descended a ladder like the Doddridge ladder, and knocked at a door on a landing, almost a duplicate of his door and landing.

Piggot opened the door, sleepy-eyed but happy at the
sight of Brad.

Piggot was slender, pale, with a slow, lopsided smile,
and hard as nails. Like Brad, he had once been a House
of Refuge child and later a street boy. With this shared
knowledge of what they had behind them, with the
joint realization that they had both risen above it,
their friendship was very close. As a matter of fact,
when you came right down to it, Piggot was still,
in a way, a street boy. Part of his duty required him to
cover the city in making deliveries for Duquesne.

The garret was rectangular, with a crude bed along
one side wall, a chair along the other, and the dormer
window, now open to the hot breeze of the summer's
night, taking up much of the other wall, the wall facing
the door. Piggot sat on the bed, Brad on the chair
against the unplastered wall.

They did a little talking, but not much. Mainly they
just sat there, silently, enjoying each other's presence.

But they were both thinking the same thing, won-
dering whether, if the Crown sent over reinforcements
for its garrisons and forts to pound across its upcoming
Stamp Act, there would really be war. There had been
mobs, and uprisings, and riots, and some of them
mighty lusty, but would the Americans really mobilize,

and arm, and drill, and all that—and fight? Just about every colonist thought they would. Just about every King's man thought they wouldn't.

Finally, Piggot said, "I want to fight. And I don't mean stand in a marketplace with a hundred dock hands and shake a useless cudgel in the air."

Brad, agreeing so deeply that he wished to change the subject, said, "What were you doing today? Delivering?"

"No. Duquesne and I were sugaring some candied ginger. And you? Muscles?"

"No," said Brad. "Mainly veins and arteries."

It was at that instant a startling thing happened. A man's face appeared in the open dormer window, at the top of the window, upside down.

It was a big, meaty face, weather-beaten and tan. The fleshy lips moved, and the face said, "Can I come in for a moment, please? I mean no harm."

Piggot, whom nothing ever seemed to ruffle or upset, said mildly, "Why not?"

Big fists appeared on either side of the face, grasping the upper windowsill, and the man's body, swinging down and in with great strength and dexterity, plummeted into the attic.

He wasn't even out of breath. He stood grinning bearishly, a squat, chunky human, rumpled, a little dirty, with burrs on his coarse yarn stockings—and you didn't get burrs in Sumatra Alley, you got them out in fields somewhere. And although he was dressed in odds and ends, he was a sailor; no doubt about that. His queue was tarred and he wore one earring, gold, set with a cheap purple garnet.

"I'm sometimes knowed as Boston Hollingsworth, if

you'll permit me to introduce myself," he said. "I'm not a beggar, but I'd sure like a crust of bread. I've been night-traveling for two days."

"And you ended up here," said Piggot. "In my bedroom."

"You always have to end up somewhere," said Boston. "And waterfronts attracts me."

"But we're not on the waterfront," said Brad.

"Close but not too close," said the man. "That's the proper thing, hey? Close but not too close."

Piggot got up, and, making no comment, left the attic.

When the man was alone with Brad, he said, "Where have I wharfed? What kind of a place is this?"

"It's a confection factory. Downstairs," said Brad. "And you haven't wharfed. You're just tacking through."

"Who am I to argue?" said the man. "You work here?"

"No," said Brad. "It's the other boy who works here."

Piggot returned. He had milk in a pint pewter mug, a piece of bread, and a generous wedge of cheese. The man devoured everything greedily.

When he had finished, he pointed to a bowl and pitcher on the floor in a corner. "I'd deeply appreciate a free wash, too."

"Go right ahead," said Piggot. "Who am I to say No?"

Boston stripped to the waist, exposing a bullish, muscular chest, and bathed. When he had finished, holding his tawdry gingham shirt limply in his big hand, he said, "I enjoyed that as much as the food, and that's a lot."

Piggot said, "I sure don't mean to pry, but I don't suppose you got anything more to tell us?"

"No," said the man softly. "Not much, that is. But I got something to show you, you might say."

He raised his arm. Just below his armpit, at the top of his rib cage, was a big, black, inky-looking letter *D*.

Neither of the boys said anything.

"This here is a present from His Royal Highness, King George the Third," said the man. "The *D* means deserter. They say I'm a deserter from His Majesty's Navy."

"I thought they burned them in, branded them in," said Piggot with interest.

"With gunpowder, sometimes," said Boston. "But generally, they don't even bother with that. They just shoot you."

"What happened?" asked Brad.

Boston put on his shirt. "I been a honest, hard-working American seaman since I was hardly the age of you young'uns," he said. "Not long ago a detail of British sailors impressed me, outside a taproom in Portsmouth, one rainy night. Which, I doubt me not, is a story both of you has heard oft many times before. They done it very ceremonial, with expensive uniforms and torches and drums. I was half-seas over at the moment. They took me aboard a frigate, and throwed me in the scuppers to sober up. I sobered up, decided I liked it better as it was before, and deserted. They caught me, give me forty lashes and my *D*, and I foxed them and got away from 'em a second time."

"And here you are," said Piggot.

"And here I am, but nobody knows for how long," said Boston. "Now I'm going to ask you a favor. Would

you give me a bit of information? Where would a stranger, a Boston man, say, go here in town to join up with
the Sons of Liberty?"

Frozen, they stared at him.

The Sons of Liberty. That network of patriotic, anti-
royal, anti-British clubs which stretched now into all
the colonies, everywhere, with New York City as a
sort of pivotal geographic point. The Sons of Liberty,
coming more and more out into the militant open, was
the one thing you didn't discuss with strangers, especially when you didn't really know anything about
it, just rumors, like everyone else.

The millionaire Hancock, and Otis, up there in Boston, and William Livingston, here in New York, could
orate their heads off in fire and brimstone in favor of
it, but these were powerful men, of position and
strength; you, if you were nobody much, just didn't
talk about it, for or against it.

"The Sons of Liberty?" said Piggot. "I wouldn't
know. What do you want with them? You want to
fight?"

"Yes, certainly, later," said Boston. "But I'll tell you
the truth. I thought first, though, they could get me
away and hide me somewhere until things cool off a
little for me. Anybody can see I'll be valuable to them
a little later on."

"What would you say, Brad?" asked Piggot.

"How would I know?" asked Brad. "No one ever tells
us boys anything. But maybe they could help you at
the Merchants Coffee House."

That was safe enough. The Merchants Coffee House
was known the breadth of the colonies as a white-hot
center of rebellion. If he went there, and asked, and

they wanted him, they would take him. And if they didn't want him, they would just look stupid. The Merchants Coffee House could take care of itself.

"I'll be going," said the man.

"You don't have to leave by the way you came," said Piggot. "By the window. Outside the door, in the hall, you'll find a landing and a ladder to the roof. Go that way. Up, not down. You go down through the house and Master Duquesne will sprinkle you with his blunderbuss. He don't much care for prowlers."

"Thank you, mates," said the man. "Good luck, and good night."

When their visitor had departed, Brad said, "Whew!"

He waited about ten minutes for the way to get clear, and then he himself left.

2

Next morning, Brad and the doctor laid aside their four-layer wax arm temporarily and prepared for the arrival of Captain Lynnwood, of the Georgia Rangers, a fiercely royal group of fighting men, who, on occasion, had acted as personal bodyguard to the fiercely royal governor of that colony. The Captain was in New York on planters' business, a little for himself, a little for the Governor, and had taken a whim to have a wax-portrait plaque of himself made during the interval. Dr. Doddridge rarely made plaques of this nature, but was quite capable of it, and, after a consultation with Brad, decided they could well use this extra financial windfall.

The doctor had eaten and had Brad's breakfast ready for him, bacon and gruel, when Brad came down the chimney staircase and out the narrow door by the fireplace. Breakfast getting was technically one of Brad's duties, but in this household each was so anxious to take any little labor off the other that duties were actually nonexistent.

Dr. Doddridge was a nervous little sparrow of a man, with a red, wrinkled, newborn-baby sort of a face, and generally with a dusting of silver stubble on cheeks and jaws, uneven and patchy, because he was totally uninterested in the mechanics of shaving. His clothes were a lumpy, mildewed green. But the heart under that slovenly waistcoat, Brad well knew, must be as big as a ship's anchor.

The workroom, when Brad had first seen it, had looked to him like a large, low raftered kitchen, with tables and stands and cupboards, and an enormous maw of a fireplace with strange-looking caldrons and cooking implements. Now, after his meager breakfast, he helped his elderly friend prepare for the arrival of their wealthy customer.

"Maybe he'll commission us for an anatomical model, too, while he's here," said Brad.

"Hardly likely, I'm afraid," said the doctor. "What he wants, and the only thing he wants, I'd say, is a portrait. A splendid mirrorlike reflection for him to study and dream over. An image of his own dazzling, exalted physiognomy."

"But he's a terror with the saber, I hear," said Brad. "And absolutely fearless."

"That's true," said the doctor. "But I can tell you one thing. You didn't hear it inside the Merchants Coffee House. His enemies try to pretend otherwise."

"I've never been inside the Merchants Coffee House," said Brad.

In good wax modeling, superfine wax was required, perfectly bleached, and Brad made it a practice to keep a store of well-bleached wax always at hand.

The crafts, all of them, had carefully guarded formulas which they treasured and called "trade secrets," to be always hidden from outsiders. The doctor had learned to bleach and work wax years ago in London from an elderly waxworker patient of his, and out of respect for him and his guild, they, too, guarded their processes and left off this hidden end of the work the moment an unexpected visitor dropped into their kitchen.

The base was high-grade beeswax that was first melted at a certain temperature which would not destroy its quality, in a caldron with a pipe at its bottom. Through this pipe, the melted wax flowed into a wooden cylinder which was always turning. The outside of the cylinder was washed with water, forming the wax into solid whitened ribands. After the wax had dried, the operation was repeated until the proper degree of perfection was obtained, and then the wax was cast into cakes. The great secret of modeler's wax was the addition of lead plaster, olive oil, resin, and whiting. The finished model was then carefully painted with oil paints, which were prepared in a mixture of wax and oil of turpentine just before being applied. In addition to having all this secret information, a modeler had to be talented and highly skilled. Brad wasn't exactly talented, or as skilled as the doctor, but he partly made up for it by concentration and steadiness.

Dr. Doddridge said, "I guess you'd better run over and get that chair now."

There was nothing in the workshop, it seemed, elegant enough for the gentleman from Georgia. On mornings of these sittings, Brad borrowed a red damask chair from Mr. Huggins, the harpsichord maker.

Brad left, and by the time he returned with the chair, Captain Lynnwood had arrived and was standing by a corner of the hearthstone, in a slightly posed posture, talking to the doctor.

He was a wiry, leathery little man, with a spiderlike saber scar on his bronzed cheek, which was as notorious as he was, and he was dressed today in very expensive, paper-thin, dove-gray wool.

The sword at his hip was a beauty, with jeweled hilt and scabbard, but Brad, who had never seen the blade itself, knew it was not a toy, a foppish dress blade, for these were days in which every man who wore a blade took care it was a workable weapon should some emergency arise. Ten to one, Captain Lynnwood's blade came out of the best armorer's in Sheffield.

Brad placed the chair by the easel with the covered plaque, and Captain Lynnwood sat down, ignoring him completely.

Dr. Doddridge removed the muslin from the plaque's face and stared at it a moment, thoughtfully. It was medal-shaped, a disk about ten inches in diameter, in low relief, almost finished. It was a good likeness all right, except that maybe, just maybe, the broken hawk-nose had been straightened a little, and the thin lips softened a little, making the face not unattractive.

As the doctor picked up his palette—a small baking sheet borrowed from neighbor Duquesne, the master confectioner—Captain Lynnwood said, "What makes the boy stand and stare?"

They went through this every time.

"He's not staring," said the doctor. "He's just being alert."

"He irritates me," said the Captain. "I do not like to be stared at. I'm not an actor, performing. Send him away."

This, too, the Captain said every time, almost in the same words.

Now the doctor came up with a suggestion. Always, at this point, though each time it was a different one.

he came up with a suggestion. One thing about the doctor, Brad realized, if you could ever get him out of the field of his precious anatomical models, and thrust him into the purely mercantile world, he went whole hog.

This time, he said, "Brad, go down to the Big Market, and bring back six nice roasting potatoes."

The Big Market, in this neighborhood, was Coenties Market, not far away.

"Need any money?" asked Captain Lynnwood, condescendingly.

"No," said Brad.

The Captain took out a little purse covered with cut steel beads, opened it, produced a sixpence, and tossed it in Brad's direction. It rolled to the wall, spun a little, and flopped on its side. "Take it anyway," said the Captain. "Buy yourself a nice raspberry tart."

Brad ignored the coin and left. The Captain always tossed a coin, Brad always ignored it, but when Brad returned, the doctor had always picked it up and pocketed it.

Once, on his return, Brad had shown his anger at this to the doctor. The doctor had said coldly, in a tone he had never used before or since, "Grow up!"

As Brad came out of Sumatra Alley onto South Street, onto the waterfront, with the towering ships at berth on his right hand and the seething of dock traffic swirling about him as he walked, he remembered a conversation he had overheard between Mr. Duquesne and the doctor about the port's tremendous growth. About three thousand houses, they'd said, and that didn't even begin to count the population that lived in basements and cellars and attics and even on the streets. Three thousand houses, and other buildings, shops and offices and taverns and stables and goodness knew what other structures going up so fast it was impossible to reckon them. New Yorkers wondered if the city wasn't bigger than Boston, even bigger than Philadelphia.

The city had five giant markets, New, Oswego, Fly, Old Slip, and Coenties—all strictly regulated under the authority of the Crown, of course. And say what you wanted to against the King, the British ran, or tried their best to run, a good, fair market. And they had to be good, and fair, for the law said that all perishable provisions, with a few exceptions, had to be sold in these markets.

The markets here were run on just about the same ironclad regulations that had governed markets in England for hundreds of years. Forestalling in any form was forbidden; that meant no market merchant, or group of market merchants, could go out in the country and stop farmers coming in with produce, and buy it in advance, cheap, where there was no competition, and bring it in and raise the prices outlandishly. Nor could a group of merchants get together and try to control the available supply of something and raise prices. For the benefit of the citizenry, the Crown tried to keep prices fair.

Then weights. Scales were tested frequently, and sealed when correct, the clerk of the market getting a nice fee for each scale he sealed, which kept him alert and greatly reduced fraud.

The big trouble with selling perishable provisions, of course, was that sometimes unscrupulous merchants sold them when they were bad. The law was merciless on this point. Bad butter was a regular offender. One merchant even put good new butter as a casing over the old putrid butter in his butter rolls, and was severely fined for it. Selling "blown," or putrid meats, was enough to bring a merchant complete financial disaster.

There was a time when this almost-everything-under-one-roof law was relaxed and little shops sprang up everywhere, away from the marketplace. But too many larcenous shopkeepers tried to make too much money too fast, at the expense of their abused customers, and the old laws were brought out again, and polished up, and reenacted.

Two years ago, an Assize of Victuals had been passed, which said:

> No kind of provisions or victuals are to be sold anywhere but in the common Market Houses of this city (except live fish, bread, flour, salted beef, salted pork, butter, milk, hog's lard, oysters, clams and Muscles) under the penalty of £40 for each offence.

Butter got in, but it was strictly supervised. No huckster could buy to sell again before 11 A.M. This was to keep hucksters themselves from forestalling, right there in the marketplace.

All markets. by law, were open every day except Sunday, from sunrise to sunset.

Some years back it had been the practice for riffraff to go in business for themselves *around* the marketplace, preying on householders attracted to the market. They bought and sold and displayed not only in neigh-

boring houses, but in shacks and outhouses and yards—
boiled corn on the cob, half-rotten fruit, and a variety
of other contaminated items. The squalor and catch-
penny thievery in these hide-by-night establishments
were beyond belief. The practice was stopped by law;
offenders were to be publicly whipped.

Weaving his way through the carts and wagons and
mounds of produce in the market square, Brad entered
the building itself, and that old feeling of pleasure
that came over him when he entered any market anywhere came over him again.

The place was enormous, and stanchions and pillars
ran up to vaulted beams overhead. Around the sides
were booths and stalls and cubicles, each with its own
particular variety of food. Though the July day was hot
and blazing with sun outside, here it was cool and
medium dim. Smells engulfed him, blended, each stall
making its contribution, and this overall smell was
inexpressibly exciting.

The items in each stall were not simply set out, but
were attractively, beautifully displayed, artistically,
because the style of display was part of that particular
trade. The clams and oysters and lobsters, in their
jewel-like shells, wore wisps of crisp green water
cress. The poulterers' booths had backdrops of hanging turkeys and geese and ducks, waxen and delicious
looking; and short, broad counters in front, with plump
plucked chickens, snowy white and golden tinted with
lush, almost bursting, fat, which were stacked like cannon balls and graded as to age and size. As in England,
beef—loins and sirloins, quarters and sides and roasts—
was displayed in the beef stalls, and pork in the pork

stalls, never together; for no beef merchant sold pork, or vice versa. Brad bought his six roasting potatoes, carefully, from a bin at the far end of the market floor.

Then, as he could never help doing—maybe it was a holdover from his hungry days on the streets—he took a quick little tour of the place, just to look.

He was standing at a counter heaped with satiny, glass-eyed fish, picking out with his judgment those that seemed to have roe in them, when a man he had never seen before jostled his shoulder in passing behind him and said, "You Brad Agnew?"

"Yes," said Brad, half questioningly, and turned.

The man was stumpy, dressed like a dock worker, and had smoky, veiled eyes. He said, "I thought I recognized you. I got something to tell you."

"You seem to know *me*," said Brad. "But I don't know you."

"By sight," said the man. "I know lots of people by sight."

"What do you want?" said Brad. "And who are you?"

"Just call me a Liberty Boy," said the man.

"A Son of Liberty?" said Brad, suddenly a little afraid.

"Yes," said the man shortly. "Let's get this over with. How well do you know Hyacinth Duquesne?"

"Not at all. I never heard the name until now."

"The candymaker in Sumatra Alley."

"Oh, Master Duquesne. Quite well."

"Do you trust him?"

"Yes, indeed."

"Does he trust you?"

"I think so. I hope so."

"Then take him this message," said the man. "The Sons of Liberty have reason to believe that he is suspect by the Crown as a dangerous rebel—and that he will be seeing a detail of soldiery before long. And that he'll be seeing the jail, and maybe even the tea ships, if he don't pack up and get out of sight somewhere. He's been informed on."

This didn't sound like the Master Duquesne Brad knew. He could hardly believe it. He said, "Anything else?"

"That's enough," said the man, and was gone.

Numb, Brad left the market, crossed the noisy dock, and turned from South Street, up into Sumatra Alley.

The narrow little street seemed, as always, sleepy and serene. There was even a cloud of sulphur butterflies, which drifted in from the nearby fields, hovering above the cobblestones.

It seemed impossible that serious trouble could ever find this peaceful, out-of-the-way pocket in the crowded city.

Seemed impossible, that is, until you remembered the man in the market, until you remembered those hot, smoky eyes.

That man hadn't lied.

3

There was no street show window in Duquesne's establishment, just a high square of London glass set in the brick wall by the door, for light. Brad pressed down the latch and entered. Although confectioneries were among those shops not encompassed by the market laws, and were allowed to operate independently, Duquesne ran no shop. His place here in Sumatra Alley was a kitchen-factory; he dealt wholesale, not retail.

The room was square, high-ceilinged, airy. Around two walls were open pine cupboards in a honeycomb of large pigeonholes, for a requirement of this trade was multiple ingredients, some used often, some used only rarely. Brad by now knew many of them by sight. The sugars: single- and double-refined, powdered, muscovado. The spices and figs and almonds. The prunes and currants and jars of syrupy raisins. And citron and fruit jellies and bars of bulk chocolate.

On either side of Master Duquesne's fireplace were ovens, for the confectioners' guild shared with the bakers' guild the privilege of producing certain cakes and puddings. Piggot wasn't in sight—out on a delivery somewhere, Brad imagined. Duquesne, with an immaculate apron tied under his chin, was at his ovens.

Brad knew what he was making—knew from the

delicious fragrance, in fact, the minute he entered. He was making gingerbread, and a special kind of gingerbread that would keep on long voyages, "sea gingerbread," much favored by sea captains who liked to live well.

The confectioner was a tall, straight man with deep-set eyes and big, furry black eyebrows. He was anti-British, and took no pains to conceal it. He had been in the French and Indian War, back in the fifties, and had survived two defeats by the English, but was more than willing to try it again. He treated Piggot, his bondboy, as though he were his favorite nephew, which was a lot different from some masters. Brad was always welcome here.

Now, silently, the Frenchman produced a huge pastry knife with a sawtooth edge, and, in a fluid motion that seemed a part of what he was doing at the moment, whacked off a chunk of gingerbread about the size and shape of a building brick, and handed it to Brad.

Brad, about to speak, smiled in thanks instead, and took a giant bite. A heaven of elixirs and spices and molasses, released hot in his mouth, surged through his very being.

Talking and eating at the same time, he delivered his message to Duquesne.

The confectioner continued busily about his duties. He seemed hardly to hear.

"You should have seen the man," said Brad quietly. "It was no joke."

Duquesne brought his mobile body to a sudden stillness. "I *have* seen the man," he said gravely. "He is a good friend of mine. We belong to the same club.

And I know, it's no joke. Know it a little better than you, mayhap."

"What are you going to do?" asked Brad.

"Follow the warning," said Duquesne. "This can be a very serious thing. I am going to follow the warning, and go."

"Go?" said Brad, shocked. "And leave this nice workshop? Leave your double-refined sugar, and almonds, and plum preserves? Just pack up and go?"

"Just pack up and go," said Duquesne. "And very little packing. And find other double-refined sugar elsewhere. I have expected this for some time."

"Where will you go, and how?"

"I will go to the island of St. Kitts, first, to confuse my trail, and then to Barbados. On the sloop of a friend of mine, *The Antigua Trader,* now at Old Slip."

"But Barbados is under British rule, and its people are said to be as English as steak and kidney pie."

"And what could be better? My name will become Ainsworth, and my new trade baking."

They stared at each other.

Brad said softly, "You must have done something mighty serious."

"These are serious times. I am a serious man."

"When are you going?"

"In a half hour. I think I have a half hour. Will you do me two favors, a small favor and a great favor?"

"Of course," said Brad. "The neighborhood is going to miss you. I'm going to miss you. Dr. Doddridge is going to miss you."

"I hardly know the doctor well enough to speak to," said Duquesne stiffly. "I like him, but I just don't know

him. I, in my turn, will miss the neighborhood, and
wretchedly."

Brad asked, "What are the two favors, sir?"

"First, Piggot," Duquesne said.

Brad blinked. He had forgotten all about Piggot in
this emergency.

"Piggot," Duquesne said. "He is to hang around on
the premises here for a while, as though he had been
deserted. Then he is to take ship for Bridgetown, Barbados, and join me. At Bridgetown he is to ask for me at
a small inn known as The Sceptre. I am leaving him
money under the mattress of his pallet."

"And the second one, the big one?" said Brad.

"My big peril will be on my walk from this workshop
to Old Slip and *The Antigua Trader*. In a half hour I
will come past your waxshop. When I am past, come
out and follow me. Follow me at about a hundred
yards. Until I reach and board *The Antigua Trader*.
Will you do that?"

"Certainly."

"At a hundred yards, you can be in no possible danger yourself."

"Why do you wish this?" asked Brad.

"I want you to see me safely aboard. If they take
me, I want you to know it. I do not want to simply
vanish."

"If you're taken, if you're arrested, whom shall I
look up and inform?"

"It's my guess it's you yourself who will be looked up.
You are in this now. Possibly by the man who spoke to
you in the market."

"I see," said Brad, feeling hollow, being deprived so

finally and so abruptly of two such good friends, Piggot and Master Duquesne. "I'd better be getting back to Dr. Doddridge with these roasting potatoes."

Captain Lynnwood, the arrogant and formidable King's fighting man of the Georgia Rangers, was gone when Brad returned to the waxshop.

The coin was gone, too, from the floor, and Brad knew the doctor had picked it up as soon as his wealthy guest had departed, and tucked it away in his old fashioned red leather purse. He was back working on the four-layer arm again. Brad laid the potatoes on a corner of a table and said, "Did you get the plaque finished?"

"Not quite," said Dr. Doddridge, tinting a knot of muscles lavender, purple, and violet, carefully giving each muscle its key color.

"How does he like it?" asked Brad, trying to keep off the bad news as long as possible.

"That's hard to say," said Dr. Doddridge. "Well enough, I think; at least he hasn't taken it from the easel and smashed it."

"How long will he be coming?"

"We're almost finished."

"I'll be glad when he's gone," said Brad. "He's mighty hard for me to stomach."

The doctor smiled gently, understandingly, but made no comment.

Brad said, "You'd better put down that brush. I've got something to tell you."

Dr. Doddridge looked quizzical, paused, and put down his brush.

"I've got two things to tell you," said Brad. "And one of them is going to jar you and you don't want to mess up your model there."

The doctor's face was grave.

"Which do you want first?" asked Brad. "The curious one, or the terrible one?"

"We'd better have the terrible one first," said Dr. Doddridge. "Do you know, Brad, that you're deathly pale?"

Huskily, Brad told him about Master Duquesne, all about him. He told him about the man in the market, and the Sons of Liberty, and the warning. He explained how Master Duquesne had expected the situation, and how he had even planned his flight; how he was going to take a sloop named *The Antigua Trader* to the Lesser Antilles, and how later Piggot was going to join him at Barbados.

"He's leaving in half an hour, hotfoot," said Brad. "Just think, leaving that nice workshop and all those delicacies to the rats and mice."

After a moment, the doctor said, "There are worse things than rats and mice. And Duquesne knows what's best for himself."

"We're going to miss him," Brad said. "He said he never really knew you, but always liked you."

The doctor looked upset. "I never knew him very well, either. But I always liked him, too. You see I get absentminded sometimes, and then people think I'm standoffish and rude."

Brad then mentioned the second favor Master Duquesne had asked for, the request that Brad should walk behind him to Old Slip, to keep an eye on things.

The doctor's wattles went fiery red at this. "He has no right to place you in such jeopardy. You're just a lad. He's treating you as though you were a man."

"He says I'm already deep into it," said Brad.

"That's true," said the doctor. "But no excuse to place you in further peril."

"I've already said Yes," declared Brad. "And I will not break my word."

"You manage your affairs very badly," said the doctor unhappily. "But so did I at your age. What was the other thing you had to tell me?"

Brad told him about the night visitor who had come into Piggot's bedroom through the window. About the man who said he was sometimes known as Boston Hollingsworth, the sailor with the garnet earring.

The doctor said, "And you and Piggot, of all people, believed that a casual visitor, any visitor, would come in the night, in such a way, through a window?"

"He explained his predicament," said Brad, flushing. It sounded pretty absurd, now that the story had got cold.

"He was a British spy," said the doctor quietly.

"But he was a deserter from the British Navy," said Brad. "I've told you about the *D* below his armpit."

"You also said it was inky black," said the doctor. "And that's exactly what it was, black ink. Put there especially for your benefit, and now washed off, I'm certain."

"But if he was a spy," said Brad, "why didn't he ask questions? He asked no questions."

"Perhaps by that time he knew most of the answers," said the doctor. "And was just doing a thorough job and picking up anything extra that might happen to be floating around. He tried to pump you, but you and Piggot wouldn't pump."

Brad looked startled. U. S. 1587621

"It's my guess," said Dr. Doddridge, "that he's an ex-pirate, or a part-time pirate, taking a little easy money from the British provost marshal. He was the one who informed on our neighbor Duquesne. You can bet your life on it."

"And according to you," said Brad, "that's what I'm doing—betting my life."

"That's right," said Dr. Doddridge.

Master Duquesne came by the open door, and passed it. He walked stiffly erect, glancing neither to the left nor right, and in his hand he carried a bulging cloth valise. The coat sleeve from his second-best jacket stuck out at the back of the valise, in such a hurry had it been packed.

As Brad walked to the door to follow him, the doctor said, "Come right back."

"Yes, sir," said Brad.

"Right back!" called the doctor, as Brad stepped out onto the cobbles.

Waiting a little, allowing the confectioner to get about a hundred yards ahead of him, Brad began to follow him.

The shortest route from Duquesne's shop to Old Slip was southwest by Sumatra Alley to South Street and Coenties Slip, as Brad had gone earlier, then northeast on South Street two short blocks, past three smaller slips, to Old Slip.

Now, at first, it seemed to Brad that Duquesne wasn't headed for Old Slip at all, but in the opposite direction. They were going not southwest but northeast.

This northeast end of Sumatra Alley tailed out after a short walk into Front Street, which crossed it broadside. Here Duquesne turned right, with Brad cautiously at his distance behind him. Never once did the confectioner seem aware of him.

Front Street ran northeast. This was a section of drab and stark buildings, not on the waterfront but waterfront in atmosphere and feeling. Man and boy, continuing along Front, passed Cuyler's Alley, proceeding yet another block, and here Duquesne came to a bustling intersection, where, at the corner, he once more turned right. Turning right would head him directly for the waterfront, and Old Slip.

It was apparent now what Duquesne had done. He had rejected the short route, the natural route, via South Street, as too public, and had taken a lengthier, oblique way through back streets. He had taken the three roundabout sides of a rectangle instead of the single direct side.

But, in a way, he was as badly off as before, for the street they debouched on, the man first, Brad following later, was a very busy thoroughfare halfway between Wall and Broad Street. It was a wide street, an esplanade almost, with Old Slip only a block away at its foot. Only a block away, but what a block.

Here the city and the water met in turmoil and confusion. The street itself, broad in cobblestones, was actually a prolongation, a sort of apron to the Old Slip dock. On either side of the street were flagstone pavements, bordered with a mix-up of mismated structures, one, two, and even three stories high. In the center of the street were wagons, drays, carts, dogs, people, and even a few bullocks.

Vendors and hawkers, some with trays suspended at their chests, some waving items of sale in their hands, wove in and out of the crowd, bawling, blowing tin whistles, chanting their wares.

Edging the flagstones on either side were ship chandlers, with anchors and huge coils of rope outside their doors; secondhand clothing shops, with oilskins hanging from lintels, and bins of muddy-looking shoes; dank stone steps leading down to evil cellar groggeries; narrow stairs leading up to cutthroat lodging rooms; hogsheads and bales, barrels and crates, kegs and boxes.

And now, Duquesne walking systematically, mechanically, he was almost to the coping of the stone slip. In the great jumble of docked craft, with their towering masts and spars and networks of hempen rigging, Brad now could see the sloop with her weathered hull, *The Antigua Trader*. She had her gangplank down, and a man with arms crossed, elbows on the gunwale, obviously an officer, judging from his hat, stared moodily out into the clamor, at nothing.

Master Duquesne had almost reached the foot of the gangplank when it happened. A small detail of British soldiers, immaculate, bright in red tunics and fastidious in pipe-clayed crossbelts, seemed to materialize around him. Two seized him by each of his arms, just above his elbows.

The officer on the deck of *The Antigua Trader*—frightened, by the look in his eyes—went rigid and did nothing.

Brad wheeled, and broke into a run. Two of the soldiers detached themselves from the group and came after him at a clumsy lope, hampered by their accouterments.

Shuttling, dodging back and forth between the carts and wagons and bullocks, Brad had made perhaps thirty feet when a heavy hand, wrenching his shoulder, brought him to a stop.

He turned to stare at his captor.

It was Boston, the big sailor with the garnet earring. He was smiling, his suety face contorted in a happy grin.

The two soldiers came rushing up, metal clinking, leather squeaking, heavy boot soles hammering on the cobbles. They relieved Boston of his prisoner, and took Brad firmly in hand.

One of them said, "Thank you, friend."

Boston, pretending bewilderment, said, "What's going on? I was just trying to save this young man's life. I was afraid he'd get run down by one of these crazy wagons."

This was ridiculous.

"He's with that man with the valise," said the soldier. "So he must be wanted by the Crown."

"Is that so?" said Boston, pretending concern. "Well, I can tell you this. I wouldn't catch no boy for no soldier, as much as I respect a soldier. I never seen this young'un before, but I'm sure he ain't guilty of nothing. Couldn't you reconsider and leave him go?"

"Afraid not," said the soldier shortly. "Duty is duty."

Just before they parted, to lead Brad back to the others and Duquesne, Brad saw Boston and one of the soldiers exchange an amused, conspiratorial wink.

4

The jail, in that section of the city known as "the fields," was only seven years old and looked new from the outside, but was already grimy and odorous inside. It was a little square building of stone, three stories high, with a cupola. It faced south, and before its entrance was a charming little picket fence and two nice big shade trees. This was the idyllic picture it presented from the front. Behind it was a new pillory, and a large wooden cage for disorderly boys who publicly broke the Sabbath. Behind the cage was the workhouse.

Brad and Duquesne, after being thoroughly searched on the ground floor, were taken upstairs to the second floor. Here Brad was placed in a large enclosed space, a sort of communal pen for derelicts and flotsam and riffraff, and Duquesne was lodged in a small windowless cell at the end of a corridor.

While they were being searched, Duquesne had repeatedly requested to know the charge against them, and had got only stony muteness in answer.

This had greatly disturbed them both, for it had shown them that the entire procedure was unofficial, hidden, and that they had left the world with their arrest on Old Slip dock and had simply vanished.

Brad's big pen was simply a long, narrow room with stone walls on three of its sides and a fretwork wrought-iron grating on its fourth, the corridor side. At intervals along its back wall were vile nests of half-rotted straw for beds. The tiny, high, dusty grilled windows let in only a grayish illumination, a slaty sort of morning twilight. The air stank. It was stale and suffocatingly hot. For the first time in years, Brad was badly scared.

He folded his arms across his chest, leaned his shoulder blades against the stone wall, and waited gloomily.

Waited for what?

The only other occupant of the iron-barred room at the moment was a scrawny old man down at the far end, in just about the filthiest rags and tatters Brad had ever seen. With nothing better to do, Brad watched him. The old man, with cracked, puffy lips and mucus-encrusted eyelids, sat cross-legged on the floor. He went on about his business, ignoring Brad.

First, he removed a horn button—which had long ago been an ornament—from the tail of his coat. Then, with painstaking patience, he unraveled a long thread from somewhere inside the coat's lining. Next, he produced a large darning needle hidden under the tongue of one of his boots (illegal in jail, and missed by the warders who searched him). Assembling all his little treasures, he sewed the button to the front of his sailcloth blouse, where it was badly needed. This finished, he replaced his needle, and seemed to lapse into a coma.

Outside in the corridor, a warder rattled the door and slid two pewter mugs through a six-inch opening at the door's bottom. The old man got up, took one of them back into his corner, and drank its contents greedily.

The one remaining, Brad knew, must be his. He left the wall, went to it, picked it up, and inspected it. It was a thin, pasty gruel giving off a nauseating smell. He stirred its contents curiously with his forefinger, dislodged something in its depths, something half solid, which he brought to the surface. It was so far gone that for the life of him he couldn't tell what it was. It was either rotted, putrid fish, or carrion pork. He dropped it quickly back into its liquid out of sight, closed his eyes, and turned his head.

The old man was watching hungrily.

Brad took it over and handed it to him.

At first, the old man refused it. Shaking his head, he said, "Much as I want it, no. If you were older, like me, and had been in and out of jails as much as I have, and knew what you were doing, I'd take it. But you don't. Eat it, even if you have to make yourself do it. I can tell you here and now it's a banquet to some of the things you'll eat here, when you eat at all."

Brad thought it over, seriously. He knew the man was talking good sense. Finally, he said, "You need it. I don't."

"If you put it that way," said the old man, grinning. "Thanks." He took it, and drank it rapturously.

All at once, as Brad stood there, looking at this pitiable wreck, he remembered something he had heard years ago, when he was a waif on the streets—that, if you wanted to know what was really happening in the city, there were two places you could learn: from the loafers at the inn stables, and from the denizens of jails.

"I'm here without charge," said Brad. "What does that mean?"

The old beggar gazed at him sympathetically. "It could mean a lot of things. It don't look too good. What's your name?"

"Bradley Agnew. I'm a waxworker's apprentice."

"Means nothing to me. Nothing at all. Who was that come in with you?"

"A man named Hyacinth Duquesne."

"What's he do?"

"He's a master confectioner in Sumatra Alley."

"Nothing there rings no bell to me. He a friend of yours?"

"Yes."

"I can't seem to get started on this. Anything else?"

"Before I answer that, I have to know your politics. How do you hold?"

"I hold with myself," the old man said.

"And with Hancock and the Independents, maybe?" said Brad hopefully.

"No."

"With King George?" asked Brad unhappily.

"No. With none of that no more. I'm too old and misbegotten. I hold only with day to day, a crust of a muffin in the gutter, and somebody's throwed-away apple core."

Brad took a chance. He said, "Master Duquesne is a Son of Liberty. He was warned by a fellow Liberty Boy to leave town immediately, that the British were after him. We were on the way to his ship when we were arrested."

"And you were walking with him?"

"A hundred yards behind him."

"Then they was after you, too, o' course," said the beggar. "What *you* been up to?"

"Nothing," said Brad.

The old man's eyes bored into his. "Be honest with me, son."

"Nothing at all," said Brad.

"You a Son of Liberty, too?"

"I follow their belief in my heart, but I don't belong. Actually, I know nothing about them."

"You see," said the begger slowly, "your friend, this Master Duquesne, wasn't arrested with all this trouble and secrecy and seriousness just because he was a Son of Liberty."

"I happen to know differently," said Brad.

"You happen to *think* you know differently," said the old man. "A Son of Liberty, if he's ordinary, is a heap of bother and maybe fright to the British, but nothing more. They gather in mobs, big and little, at the drop of a hat, and yell their defiance, and give tax masters a hard time, but over in England the Crown, when you come right down to it, is mighty careful not to throw no real spark in the powder keg. Of course sometimes some of their firebrand officers, like Colonel James here at the fort, says the rebels should be rode down by the English Imperials like foxes. And that the stamp tax should be crammed down their throats with his swords, but just says it and is careful not to do nothing."

"Then I don't understand it," said Brad.

"Recall I said the Crown don't want to throw no spark in the powder keg?"

"Yes."

"Well, that privilege ain't confined to the Crown, and the Crown by now mighty well knows it. It don't want no rebels throwing in that spark, neither."

Brad said, "But what's this got to do with Master Duquesne? He's the last man in the world to throw in that spark."

"We'll get back to Master Duquesne in a minute.

First we'll talk a little more about these Sons of Liberty. The movement is spreading like wildfire. Every colony, even those colonies so loyal to the Crown, has its Sons of Liberty boys in it, somewhere. The time could come when these men arise, and what would Colonel James with his hundred-and-fifty-one men here at the fort do then?"

"He could fire those big British cannon."

"They're big, I'll grant you that. But can they reach down to Georgia, say, or up to New Hampshire? He could fire his cannon but it would be unwise."

While Brad thought this over, and remained silent, the old man said, "The thirteen colonies stretch north and south along the Atlantic Coast, don't they? And while New York City ain't in the center, it's sure enough the hinge between north and south. It's from here in New York City that all these feelers spread out that make King George so unhappy."

"It could well be," agreed Brad.

"It's my guess that they spread out mainly from one man. And from what you've just said, I think that man is your Master Duquesne."

Brad smiled and shook his head. "It couldn't be, not Master Duquesne. He talks anti-British sometimes, but no one ever gives it a second thought. Master Duquesne is just a candymaker."

"And what could be more peaceful and harmless than a candymaker?" said the old man mildly.

"Right!" said Brad emphatically. "And if you knew him, you would know this is true."

He thanked the old man for his rambling, fumbling attempt to help, and returned to his end of the long room. When he next glanced in that direction, the old man had snuggled down in a heap of straw, and was contentedly asleep.

He himself settled down, not on the dirty straw, but on a bare patch of flooring, cross-legged, his shoulders against the stone back wall, and after an hour or so, drowsed.

He was awakened by a harsh, throaty whisper, which said urgently, "Brad! Brad Agnew, there!"

He opened his eyes quickly.

A man stood beyond the wrought-iron grille in the corridor. Despite the oppressive heat of the summer day, he wore a voluminous stage driver's winter cape, which muffled his cheeks and ears and dropped to his boot tops; a bottle-green garment, shoddy and wrinkled. His black tricorn hat was pulled down on the bridge of his nose, and all you could see between cape collar and hatbrim was a pair of little gimlet eyes. At first Brad thought he was a complete stranger, and then, his ear echoing back to him that voice, he knew him. It was the man who called himself Boston Hollingsworth, the sailor, the man who had caught him for the soldiers, who was responsible for his being here.

Brad got up and walked over. He said curiously, "Did you call me, Mr. Hollingsworth?"

Recoiling in surprise, a little too much surprise to be convincing, Boston said, "Don't tell me people can reckernize me in this getup!"

"More important to me," said Brad, "is how you knew my name. You called me Brad Agnew."

"I made it my business to find out," said Boston. "I done you an accidental injury and am getting ready to make up for it."

From beneath his cape his big, scaly, dirt-encrusted hand came out with a large brass key; he thrust it through an interstice of the grille, and held it there. Brad ignored it.

"Take it," said Boston. "And be quick about it. It unlocks the cell door here."

"And how came you by it?" said Brad.

"Let's say I bought your warder a Christmas goose," said Boston.

"Let's say I take it," said Brad. "And walk out, and down the stairs. What about the other warders I have to pass through on the ground floor?"

"Let's say I bought Christmas geese all around," whispered Boston. "And jest remember one thing. If it was ole Boston, through a regrettable mistake, got you in, it was ole Boston, through considerable expense, who got you out."

Careful not to touch the key, Brad said coldly, "Go back to where you came from, wherever it was. I want none of this."

Boston dropped the key inside, on the floor. "You may change your mind," he said. Threateningly, he added, "And you better. They got something terrible in store for you!"

When man and cape had vanished down the corridor, Brad kicked the key along the floor, to the grille, and outside. He didn't want to change his mind, to be later tempted.

The key lay golden on the corridor floor.

Brad returned to his little place along the back wall.

The old beggar on his straw began to snore, softly. Whatever his dreams were, they must have satisfied him, for he was smiling a little.

A few minutes later, the putty-faced jail warder came down the corridor from the direction of the stairhead. He picked up the key negligently as he passed it and put it in his pocket as though it didn't exist, and, without breaking his stride, continued in the direction of Master Duquesne's cell.

A moment later he reappeared, with Master Duquesne, walking straight and erect and entirely composed, beside him. As he passed Brad's door, he unlocked it (with the same adventurous key), said curtly, "Out." Then: "Come along."

Brad stepped out and joined them. The warder relocked the door. The old beggar on his straw was awake now. He grinned farewell.

Duquesne, looking straight ahead, said only, "You all right, Brad?"

"Yes, sir," said Brad. "What's happening?"

No one answered him.

They went down the stairs, turned back into a little cross corridor behind the stairwell, and entered a small white plastered room bare of anything but a big varnished table and a few cane-bottomed chairs. Captain Lynnwood, of the Georgia Rangers, now in peacock-blue brocade, stood elegantly alone, his hawklike face pinched in distaste, as though the very air were contaminated. The warder gestured them across the threshold and left them.

"You're free," Captain Lynnwood announced indifferently.

"Due to what?" asked Master Duquesne suspiciously.

"Due to me," said Captain Lynnwood.

"Then I suppose I should thank you," said Master Duquesne, a lack of warmth in his voice.

"Don't bother," said Captain Lynnwood, bored. "Goodness knows, it wasn't my idea."

"Whose idea was it?" asked Duquesne.

"Dr. Doddridge's," said Captain Lynnwood. "He was distressed over the boy here. You were included more or less by accident."

"How did you do it?" asked Brad.

Captain Lynnwood said, "The Governor of New York and the Governor of Georgia are close friends. I am not unknown to the Governor of New York. When the doctor brought his request to my attention, I took the necessary steps."

"May I ask why you were so moved?" said Brad.

"You may indeed," said Captain Lynnwood. "The portrait plaque is unfinished. In his great anxiety, Dr. Doddridge's quivering hands were in no state to finish it."

"Now there is a humane, unselfish reason if I ever heard one," said the confectioner, his mouth agape in repugnance.

Captain Lynnwood, impassive to this remark, said, "Doubtless, courtesy demands that I offer to send you back to your home in my carriage. May I offer this?"

"I'll walk," said Master Duquesne.

"How about you, young fellow?" asked Captain Lynnwood.

"I'll walk too," said Brad. "But thank you, sir. I want to get the memory of the sight and smell of a certain mug of gruel upstairs out of my mind."

Master Duquesne and Brad bowed and left him. Captain Lynnwood bowed in response; civilized deportment demanded it of him. But it was barely a phantom of a bow, a shadow of a bow, short, quick, uncommunicative, as though an invisible pistol were at his temple.

Outside, as Brad made his way with his companion back to Sumatra Alley, he knew suddenly, with a shock, that he had spent much more time in that wretched jail than he had realized, for purple dusk was already veiling doorways and eaves and harsh cobblestones. The hour of the lamplighters had come and gone, and here and there, as they passed along, bulbs of effulgence, feeble and thin, spluttered above their heads. Brad told the intently-listening candymaker about the sailor Boston, about both adventures with him.

"You used very good, very mature judgment," said Master Duquesne. "You had a close call."

"Close call?"

"If you had taken his key and had got out, he'd always have had a hold on you. You would have got out of the jail all right—that had been all fixed up for him by the people he works for—but you, henceforth, would have been tight in his talons."

"But why would he, or anybody else, for that matter, want me in his talons? I'm nobody."

For the next five minutes, neither of them spoke. Finally, Brad said, "Well, I'm glad it's all over."

In a tight voice, Duquesne said, "Over? Well, well!"

Now silence engulfed them as they walked. The feeling of companionship was still there, but changed somehow, intensified, and blended with a feeling of dread.

5

July went into August, August into September, and nothing, nothing whatever, further occurred to disturb the tranquillity of Sumatra Alley. Within a month, the experience of the jail was tempered to almost nothing in Brad's young and always busy mind, but somehow, separate from the vanishing memory, the feeling of unexplainable dread came back to him occasionally, and at odd times. Things at the confectionery seemed to go on exactly as before, Master Duquesne flying around, producing those marvelous pastries and sweetmeats. The store was thriving, thought Brad.

His attitude toward Brad, however, had changed. He became restrained and cool to Brad, but Brad realized that this was an effort to separate himself from Brad in the eyes of the world, for Brad's protection.

Brad and Piggot, on the other hand, became even more friendly, with a deep and increasing loyalty to each other. Captain Lynnwood's plaque was finished, and he returned with it to his rangers, and the service of the King, down in Georgia. A hospital in Boston placed a big order for nine anatomical models, and the doctor, who enjoyed the onus of hard work, became deliriously happy. Brad's systematic instruction under his mentor continued satisfactorily, and in his medical studies he progressed from febrifuges to diaphoretics and astringents.

One day, early in September, Brad said, "I wonder what ever became of that man Boston? I sure have him on my mind."

"Who can say what became of a ruffian like that?" answered Dr. Doddridge. "He may be in Madagascar, in that pirate colony there. Or he may be somewhere in the Indian Ocean with a patrolling frigate, manning a thirty-pounder for our King. It's my guess you'll probably never see him again."

But the doctor was wrong. Brad saw him the very next morning, under remarkable circumstances.

About an hour before noonday lunchtime, Dr. Doddridge, who had been out in the town on some trifling business, came in through the street door with a luscious-looking anvil-sized sweet potato under his arm. He immediately nested the potato in the hot ashes of the fireplace. Both Brad and the doctor were especially fond of sweet potatoes; for the next hour it sizzled and popped off its fragrance as they worked. When the clock said twelve, and the potato was nicely done, Dr. Doddridge said, "Brad, let's do something grand. This is Thursday. Get a pan and go around to Merkle's. Let's do our potato honor."

Merkle's was a small bakeshop which, as a sideline, supplied coarse, wonderful lunches to the dock hands of the nearby waterfront. On Thursdays, for a halfpenny, you could get a bowl of roast-pork slabs in clove gravy, plus three giant cracked-wheat muffins. Brad grinned, picked up the pan, and left.

Out on Sumatra, he headed toward South Street, but when he came to the little opening in the wall that led into the arched-over passage, he decided to take the shortcut and turned in. This passage, winding, stinking,

windowless, was grandly named Queen Anne Lane.
Midway its length, you came suddenly into a rubbish-
strewn open area surrounded by tiny, seamy shops.
This place, too, had a grand name: Queen's Court. That
was its official name, but it was known to certain
informed persons as Smugglers' Row; in these days of
taxes and hardship, smuggling was an honored profession. To yet other people, even a little better informed,
its true name was Thieves' Market. Here, you could buy
almost anything you wanted, from fine inlaid dueling
pistols to a lady's tiara, but the business of buying, as
well as the business of selling, was very touchy and
complicated.

For a small gold coin, Brad knew from the old days,
you could get an enemy's throat cut here. Or could get
your own throat cut, on the spot, free.

Brad, walking through the middle of the court, had
about halfway crossed it to the lane mouth that
egressed and once more became a passage at the far-
ther side, when a harsh voice from behind him said in
his ear, "Start running away from me, and I'll break both
of your legs!"

How well he knew that voice by now. By now he almost knew, too, the foul breath that went with it.

He turned and saw the sailor with the tawdry earring. Boston. His air of false jollity was gone. His meaty
face was creased unpleasantly, maliciously. Whatever
business was on his mind, he meant to take care of it
and no nonsense. He said, "Let's go over and sit down
somewheres. I'd like a little chat with you."

"Some other time," said Brad, not much liking the
tone of command in the man's words. "I'm on my way to
Merkle's to get our lunch."

"Some other time to that," said Boston. "Don't try my patience. This is mighty important to me."

Important was right, Brad decided. He had been paid to gather certain information and deliver it, probably; and had been paid, probably; and his employers, the British provost marshals, weren't satisfied.

This was a dangerous and desperate man, Brad realized. And if he were blocked, flatly blocked, he could be capable of any kind of violence, right here, right now. The way to handle this man was to outthink him. Brad said, "I'm an apprentice, and I've got a mighty bloodthirsty master. They tell me he's lost three bondboys in the past. If I'm late, it'll mean the bull-whip for me. But I'll spare you ten minutes. Will ten minutes do you?"

"Easy," said Boston, and that old forced look of jollity came back into his face. Brad liked him better the other way.

He followed the man diagonally across the court, to a door set in an otherwise blank wall. On the door, painted in yellow and red and blue, was the torso of a bearded man with bulbous muscles, holding a sledge-hammer. "The sign of the Anchor Smith," said Boston. "A tavern many have never heard of."

Brad had heard of it. He said nothing.

Inside was a square room into which daylight never came, golden and smoky now, at noon, from the light of four whale-oil lamps. Down one side of the room, at Brad's right, ran a waist-high railing with a gate, and beyond it was an assortment of the worst kind of worn-out garments and household utensils and broken crockery and furniture that Brad had ever seen offered for sale. Left of the railing, on their side, was the taproom,

ghostly and empty at this off-hour. They seated themselves at a table against the wall. "You wouldn't care to
stand me a mug of ale?" said Boston hopefully. "To
join us in brotherhood, you might say? I'm a little
short of money at the moment."

"So am I," said Brad briefly. "Well, here I am. What
do you want?"

"First, let's say I'm mighty glad I got you out of that
jail, safe and sound."

"You didn't get me out," said Brad. "And you mighty
well know it. Another party got me out."

"Well, let's say I laid the groundwork," said Boston,
trying to save something out of it, anything.

"Let's say you had nothing whatever to do with it,"
said Brad amiably. "Don't tell me that's what you
wanted to talk to me about."

"No," said Boston. "Not that." He looked moody for
a moment, then said, "I been asking a few questions
about you. I ain't learned much, but I learned one thing
important. They been right questions in the right places.
I learned it ain't likely you're one of them Sons of
Liberty. Right?"

Brad said nothing.

Boston pressed him. "Ain't that right? Will you
swear to me, right now, that you ain't?"

"I'll swear to you nothing," said Brad. "You look
mighty ugly when you say their name. A couple of
months ago, when I first talked to you, you were hot to
join them, or said as much. When did you have this
change of heart?"

"I didn't have no change of heart. I was agin them
then, and I'm agin them now. But what was I to think,
you and your friend there at Duquesne's. Duquesne

the rebel. O' course, I know different now about you two boys."

Things were moving too fast here, too fast, too permanently, too seriously.

"I don't like this conversation," said Brad.

"Rebellion or the Crown," said Boston. "The Crown or Rebellion. In these days they ain't no middle ground. You ain't for Rebellion. That means you're for the Crown."

Stunned, Brad listened.

"Ain't that only reasonable and logical?" asked Boston.

When Brad simply sat speechless, Boston said, "Son, you're a hard nut to crack. But I've finally got you figgered."

"Figured how?" asked Brad, and his voice was so confused that he hardly recognized the sound of it as his own.

"You're a loyal royalist, just an eager youngster sitting there amongst his rebellious enemies, you might say, keepin' his own counsel, his soul and elements cryin' out in misery to do a good turn for his sovereign, and the Empire. Right? It simply can't be no other way."

"Wrong," said Brad.

"That's it," said Boston. "Be careful. Don't trust nobody. Not even me."

"I hear you want to be a doctor," said Boston, after a pause. "How would you like maybe to go to a college and study it?"

"I don't know," said Brad, wary at this turn of events. "Where?"

"In Scotland, say. Where they have the best."

"I'm studying now. Under Dr. Doddridge, and he's the best."

"In your opinion, maybe."

"I couldn't bear to be separated from him," said Brad, fascinated by the amazing idea.

"Who is to say you couldn't take him with you? At no expense to either of you."

"And who would foot this bill?"

"They ain't no bill as yet. So far we're just sort of talkin'. But if it come to the point they was a bill, the British Government *might* do it."

Brad knew now that he was lying through his teeth. His big jowls were oily, sweaty, his big bloated lips were wet and smiling, but his tiny eyes were slate-hard.

On an impulse, Brad pretended to be vaguely interested. He said, "The British Government doesn't throw its money around for nothing. What am I supposed to do?"

"We'll get to that later," said Boston, persuasively now that he thought he was making ground. "We, them and me, know you as a lad of principle who likely wouldn't care to be corrupted for outright gold. Or would you? Would you like to arrange the gold instead?"

And you can't even arrange enough gold to buy yourself an ale, thought Brad. He simply waited.

At first seeming to switch the subject, Boston said, "One of the most dangerous rebels in the colonies lives in Sumatra Alley. Did you know that?"

"Who?"

"Not Duquesne. Duquesne's not dangerous, just bothersome."

"Then who?" Brad knew these people, all of them, personally. It just didn't make sense.

"It could be a goldbeater named Lundy or a harpsichord maker named Huggins."

The images of these two men came into Brad's mind: Lundy, earnest, religious, with his hands as dexterous as a violin maker's; Huggins, submerged in children and wanting more. Boston couldn't be right.

Boston said, "If I had my way about it, I'd drag His Majesty's biggest siege gun into that Sumatra Alley and blow the whole place to dust and rubble, buttons and finger rings and shoe soles."

It was a vicious thing to say, and he said it in a vicious way.

"But that won't never happen," Boston said. "That ain't the way His Gracious Majesty does things. He looks on you American colonists, us American colonists, like his children. You spank an annoying child to teach him a little lesson, but you don't destroy him. Growed children later proves useful to their parents."

"But Sons of Liberty are almost ordinary these days," said Brad. "And a lot of them don't even try to hide it. You go down on the dock and ask, and I bet the first man you meet will admit it, openly. Would you turn your siege gun on him?"

"He's bottom layer," said Boston. "They come in layers. There wouldn't be no bottom layer if there wasn't a top layer. Will you do it?"

"Do what?"

"Work on this Lundy-Huggins problem. Poke around a little. Keep your eyes and ears open. Report to me here at the sign of the Anchor Smith when you learn something. The people here will always be able to find me."

So that explained why he had tried to ensnare Brad at the jail that time. He wanted to use him as a spy.

Anger choked Brad. He was unable to pretend any longer. He said, "No."

Boston looked incredulous, then brutish.

A lazy potman came up to their table and said, "Kin I serve you gentlemen?"

Brad picked up his pan. "Nothing for me," he said. "I'm just leaving."

6

They ate their meal of roast pork and gravy and sweet potato, and all through it Brad said nothing of his experience in Smugglers' Row. He did this because, although he could put it into words all right, he knew he could never put his feelings about it into words, and he realized it was a sure thing that the doctor would come out of the conversation with his own interpretation, which could well be way off the mark. The doctor was like a father, maybe even closer than a father, but like any other father he sometimes thought on a different plane, and could be dead set in his judgments.

The thing to do, Brad decided, was to talk it over with Piggot, and as soon as possible. Piggot was his own age, was his friend, and, most important of all, he had a way of agreeing almost entirely with Brad's most casual opinions. Almost.

Piggot was very satisfactory to talk to, even just to be around.

He asked the doctor if he could have the afternoon off, and the doctor, giving him a hard look, reading an urgency in him, said of course, as though it were a normal thing.

Master Duquesne, when Brad came into his kitchen, was shaping colored fondant at a table. He spoke no word of greeting to him, but jerked his thumb toward the rear. Brad, following his directing, entered the immaculate storeroom and a back annex.

Piggot, his peaked street-boy face absorbed in his work, was removing certain articles from shelves and stowing them neatly in hampers and baskets. He was, Brad knew, about to set out on an afternoon of deliveries. He nodded at Brad, his fingers counting, recounting, his eyes searching the shelves. Piggot liked work, and when he worked, he worked utterly. Brad said, "I want to go with you on your rounds this afternoon."

"I'm afraid not," said Piggot crisply.

Taken aback, Brad said, "You mean you don't want me?" He had gone with his friend on deliveries before, only rarely, to be sure, but had always been welcomed cordially.

Piggot, all at once sorry for his answer, said, "Of course I want you. It's just that this particular trip is going to be mighty long and tiresome."

"I've got to talk to somebody," said Brad. "Got to."

"Well, that's different," said Piggot. "I always like to listen. Now let's see if I've got this straight." He began checking the baskets and hampers. "Merchants Coffee House: capers, olives, Lisbon lemons, Turkey figs, ground ginger, sweet oil, East India mangoes, anchovies, pickled cucumbers. All present and accounted for. That's the big one. Next, the *Abigail Edwards*—"

Brad blinked, but said nothing. The Merchants Coffee House, that hotbed of Independence, had roused his attention. And then came this one, the *Abigail Edwards*. He knew the *Abigail Edwards* well by sight; she was a "hulk," an immobile, dismantled ship tied at the foot of Seely Street, used, like others of her kind, her cruising days over, as a cheap place for storing, as a sort of warehouse. What would the *Abigail Edwards* be doing ordering supplies from Duquesne's?

And the supplies themselves turned out to be mildly astonishing.

"Plum cake," said Piggot, ticking it off on his fingertips. "Cask of strawberry preserves, cask of pickled walnuts, both small, catsup, pepper-sauce herrings. All present and accounted for."

Who would ever think an old wreck of a warehouse would be using such deluxe, epicure foods? It was almost as though somebody were giving a party for somebody.

The lists to other addresses went on. Finally, Piggot said. "I guess that's it. All of it. Except, of course, Mr. Huggins' barley-sugar candy."

Now Mr. Huggins, of all people, came into the picture. "Mr. Huggins?" said Brad. "I'd think Master Duquesne's products would be a little extravagant for him."

"Always, once a week, barley-sugar candy for his children. We give him a ruinous cheap price on them."

"Anything for Mr. Lundy, the goldbeater?" hazarded Brad.

"No," said Piggot. "No customers here in Sumatra Alley but Mr. Huggins. Why Lundy? I can't make any sense out of that one."

"Neither can I," said Brad. "Forget it."

Piggot put on a clean ankle-length apron, his badge of office whenever he went out officially into the town with his handcart. Together, Brad and Piggot carried the baskets and hampers out the back door and placed

them in the cart, a roomy, light vehicle with a pole at
its rear with a cross-T handle, a boxlike woven wicker
bed, and high carriage wheels for mobility, for easy
pushing. When they were out front, on the stones, on
Sumatra, Piggot pushing, Brad walking beside him,
Piggot said, "What was it you wanted to talk to me
about?"

And now Brad wavered. That strange list of customers disturbed him. He wasn't sure just what he was
into.

"We'll talk about it later," he said. "Maybe tomorrow. It wasn't much."

"This is as good a time as any," said Piggot.

"Later," said Brad.

Mr. Huggins' workroom was the last building in the
alley, on the left, where the alley came to an end at
South Street and the dock. One thing you could be
certain of, if it was daylight at all, anywhere between
sunrise and sunset, there would always be children
playing in front of it. And what a number and mixture
of them. When they were seven or over, you could tell
whether they were boys or girls from the way they were
dressed. But under that age, dresses and pantaloons
and pants and jackets were worn indiscriminatively, as
though somewhere within the house there were a big
bin of clothes and when the youngsters awoke in the
morning they went to that bin and put on whatever
they happened to grab out. They were mighty nice,
though, clean, polite, and well trained; maybe a little
overtrained, when you came right down to it, for
when you passed they were likely to yell thank-you at
you when you hadn't given them anything, or step back
out of your way and stand at military attention, when

they hadn't been in your way at all. Brad had a deep affection for the whole household.

He hated to think there was any possibility at all of an animal like Boston being on their trail.

When the cart stopped in the midst of his offspring before his door, Mr. Huggins came out and greeted them. He was a splayfooted little man, hunched, with deeply socketed eyes, a man of few words. This day, however, when Piggot handed him the candy, and he took it, he said, "Piggot, come inside a minute. I want to show you an acanthus leaf I just carved." He said "Piggot," not "boys"; Brad was pretty obviously excluded.

Mr. Huggins was not an unkind man, but he was an odd man. It could mean nothing at all.

When they started in, Brad joined them. Piggot said, "One of us better wait outside, to guard the cart."

Brad waited outside.

It took Piggot about ten minutes to look at that wood carving.

When he returned, he said, "Mr. Huggins is a wonderful carver. You ought to look at that acanthus leaf sometime."

"I'd like to," said Brad sarcastically. "If you think you can get me a special invitation."

Around the corner on South Street, about six blocks away, was Seely Street, and this Piggot selected as his next stop. The *Abigail Edwards* was berthed at her customary place, and would be berthed there, Brad knew, until somebody bought her for scrap lumber, if anyone at all could be persuaded to buy such worm-eaten scrap lumber. She was an old sloop, worn out and paintless, her hull planking now a soft gray. And that

was all she was, hull, deck, and a fairly large dilapi-
dated aftercabin—nothing more. Spars, mast, rigging,
all that had long ago been cleared away and sold.
She had three holds apparently, for hatch covers and
coamings for three hatches were visible, and this was
why she had been given a few extra years in her senility
—for the warehouse space in her holds.

There was a man, an elderly scarecrow of a man,
with thick spectacles and a massive cucumber of a nose,
standing in the sun on the deck, by the corner of the
cabin. He wore a poor man's clothes, but a rich man's
shiny black, expensive shoes. He was way out of place
on the deck of such a vessel, unless he owned it, say.
By his ankle was a strapped portmanteau, bulging.
From the luggage, Brad decided he had just arrived
or was just getting ready to leave—you couldn't tell
which, of course.

Piggot slung two hampers by their ropes crisscross
his shoulders, said, "Guard the cart," and walked up
the gangplank to the sloop's deck.

He walked directly to the man, stood for a moment
in conversation with him, and put down the hampers.

When Piggot returned to the cart, Brad said, "I don't
believe I ever saw that gentleman before."

"Not too likely," said Piggot. Then, easing a little in
his stiffness to his friend, he added, "If you can keep a
secret—but don't ask me why—he's from Philadelphia."

After this, the conversation seemed really to thin out
between them. Piggot became moody. The idea grew on
Brad that the old man, even in Piggot's brief conversation with him, had said something that disturbed
Piggot, and asked him if this was so, but Piggot simply
yanked his head No.

It was just at sunset when they came to the Merchants Coffee House.

It looked sedate, innocent, in the powdery pink sunglow, but more insurrection had been hatched here, the British claimed, than any place you could name.

Three youngish gentlemen, dressed pretty much in the foppish style, from gold-laced cocked hats and blued wigs feathery from the curling tongs through embroidered waistcoats and silken knee breeches to tiny black-glazed pumps, sat at a table near the door. They were pretty hard to look at; a lot of hours, good honest hours, had been spent here in elegant self-adornment. Maybe too many to be realistic, he suddenly decided. What were they doing there, dressed that way? Maybe they were playing a role. Maybe he was looking too hard at the clothes and not hard enough at the men. He looked harder at the men. Each of them was iron hard and leathery jawed.

Piggot took the coffee-house hampers and baskets out of the cart and put them on the flags. Then—by rope and strap and handle—he carried them, over his shoulders, under his arms, in his fists, toward the coffee-house door. His frail body staggered under the load. Brad watched him go.

This time, too, before Piggot had left, he had said, "Watch the cart. I'll be right back."

When Piggot passed the table with the three dandies, one of them spoke to him. He swerved, joined them, and put down his load, looking courteous, expectant. They spoke in a group to him; he answered. Soon, to Brad's astonishment, a fiery and friendly conversation seemed to be in progress.

It was very strange that these should converse with a humble bondboy with such cordiality and equality.

Now, out of the coffee-house door, came a rotund man, evidently the establishment's host, followed by a tough little guttersnipe youngster, obviously one of his lesser servants. Between them, they carried the gentlemen's elegant and savory-looking supper—breads, savories, a haunch of lamb, and a beef roast. On their heels came a rough-looking pantryman with a boiled duck on a silver platter. Then, as the table was set with napery and flashing silverware and the food placed upon it, a warm and relaxed discussion sprang up among everyone—Piggot, gentlemen, host, servant, pantryman.

Brad wouldn't have been too surprised to see each of the outsiders pull up a chair and join the meal. Piggot, however, simply turned away after a moment, left the baskets and hampers apparently forgotten where he had dropped them, and rejoined Brad and the cart.

Neither of them spoke of the incident. They left.

In the next hour, night came, a hot, steamy autumn night, and in that hour they made two more stops, a reeking little oyster house with opaque bubble-glass windows, the last place in the world you would think people would be interested in deluxe confections, and at an impressive three-story, mansard-roofed mansion on upper Broadway, where you'd think they would be interested—except, as Brad had been told countless times, Duquesne's didn't retail, just wholesaled.

On their walk back to Sumatra Alley with the empty cart, when Brad could stand it all no longer, he said, "I thought I was your friend?"

"You are," said Piggot. "My best friend. In fact, my only friend."

"'Then why have you been mixing me up in this, all this?"

"In what?"

"I don't know," said Brad. "But nobody can do me this way. I'm mighty sure going to find out."

"Find out, how?"

"By backtracking tomorrow where we've been today. And asking a few questions."

For a minute, Piggot said nothing. Then, not looking at him, but looking straight ahead as he walked, he said carefully, "First, I didn't ask you along. You asked yourself along. There were certain stops I had to make, and I had to make them today. Do you understand that?"

"If you say so," said Brad. "But what have we been up to?"

"Can I bind you under an oath?"

"Yes," said Brad.

"I'm a Sons of Liberty messenger boy. I can get everywhere. I can carry their messages for them."

For a moment, Brad was speechless. Finally, he said, "How long have you been doing this?"

"Long enough. They just bring me in to carry the important ones."

"And today we've been carrying an important one?"

"I'd say so," said Piggot. "You see, they can't make up their minds. They can't decide whether to take the fort, or just to scare the daylights out of it."

"Take the fort!" said Brad.

Attack Fort George! Attack the British flag, a British garrison!

"Some say Yes, some say No," said Piggot. "But I have an idea, the way feeling is going, they'll do it."

"I liked Master Duquesne," said Brad, worried. "But now I don't know. Getting a boy like you to take his chances for him."

"Master Duquesne has nothing to do with this," said Piggot. "He knows nothing whatever about it. He's just, you might say, rank and file. Rabid on the subject of Independence, but really nothing more."

Brad told Piggot about the man in the market once more, about how worried he had been about the candymaker's safety. "He said Master Duquesne was in serious, mighty serious trouble. And when Master Duquesne heard about it, he agreed."

"Serious," said Piggot. "But mayhap not quite so serious as he and his friends thought. This thing is working on levels." Brad remembered Boston and his "layers."

Piggot said, "I'm responsible to men Master Duquesne might not even know about and I daresay there's others higher than them. Taking or burning a fort, or even trying to, isn't child's play."

"Burning!" said Brad, stunned.

Now, in a burst of speech, Brad told about his visit with Boston at the sign of the Anchor Smith.

"I thought at the time it was Mr. Huggins he was after. Now I know it wasn't It isn't a man he's after, it's a boy. You."

"I'll inform them at the *Abigail Edwards,*" said Piggot.

"The *Abigail Edwards?*"

"That's where I get my instructions," said Piggot.

"From the out-of-town people, mainly, that come and go there, it *could* be headquarters."

Jarred, Brad walked numbly beside his friend. Piggot of all people, whom he had thought he knew so well.

The idea came to Brad now that he was like a person in the middle of a cyclone. You knew there was terrific motion in a circle all around you, but here, where you were, in the center, things were deathly still, uneventful.

He said, "How are they going to try to take and maybe burn Fort George? Smuggle a few good men inside?"

"They're going to try it from the outside, like you would any other fort, by assault."

"You mean an army?" said Brad in disbelief. "I hadn't heard we had any army."

"Call it what you like."

"How many men?"

"Thousands."

"Thousands?" said Brad. "You're joking."

"Wait and see."

When Piggot talked in that voice, he was always telling the truth.

Something huge was under way. How could any thing like this happen and Brad had heard no word of it, not the slightest rumor?

7

Days, weeks, went by and there was no
attack on the fort. Brad, in his instinctive consideration
for his friend, was careful never to mention this fact to
Piggot. They saw each other frequently, as before, got
along as well as ever, but the memory of that afternoon
—Brad's realization of the boyishness of Piggot's words
and looks and gestures, and the immense significance
of his hidden private life—had dropped a shadow between them. They not only never spoke of the attack
on the fort, but neither was there any allusion to Boston, or even the Sons of Liberty, from that day on.

On a tangy, purple night toward the last of October,
with the winter's first two heavy frosts already come
and gone and coal peddlers and kindling peddlers
already rapping at back doors, Dr. Doddridge sent
Brad to Mr. Lundy, the goldbeater, with an old goose-
down quilt. Mr. Lundy, whose mind seemed to dwell
only on his very skilled craft, slept in his drafty attic,
and unless he was yearly reminded of the transition
from autumn to winter, the doctor said, he was apt
to half freeze to death in these early icy nights.

Mr. Lundy's workshop was across the alley from
Mr. Huggins and had a similar front door, but there
the similarity ceased. Within the Huggins door were
workbenches loaded helter-skelter with fine carving

tools, infant garments, tuning forks, and toys. Within Mr. Lundy's door were benches, implements, tools— all shipshape, arranged in meticulous order, each in its proper place. Mr. Huggins made harpsichords to get money to feed a battery of hungry mouths. Mr. Lundy beat gold because he couldn't help it, because gold-beating with its exactness and painstaking precision was a delirium with him. That day at the tavern of the Anchor Smith, Boston had classed Mr. Lundy as a pos-sible dangerous rebel. To the denizens of Sumatra Al-ley, Mr. Lundy had a reputation of being a fanatic King's man. Someone had said Mr. Lundy couldn't be any more loyal to the Crown unless King George him-self happened to be master goldbeater.

Mr. Lundy was hard at work as usual when Brad came in. Brad put the quilt on the floor by the door, and watched, fascinated, as always.

A goldbeater made gold leaf, those almost impos-sibly thin sheets of gold used in decoration, as let-tering in tavern signs, as armorial bearings on coach doors, as gilt on expensive French-style cabinets.

There were three stages, Brad knew, for if you were an attentive listener, Mr. Lundy liked to talk about his craft when he was at rest.

In the first stage, a very thin sheet of cut gold was placed between sheets of vellum three inches square, and beaten. Two ounces of gold here produced about a hundred and seventy pieces. The packet was then un-bound, each sheet divided, placed between pieces of goldbeater's skin which was composed of cow intes-tines, and beaten again. Again the gold was divided, again beaten between goldbeater's skin. Finally, when it was all over, the two ounces of gold produced about twenty-eight hundred pieces of gold leaf each five inches square. When they were finished, they were so thin and fragile that they would almost rip if you looked at them, but Mr. Lundy, by blowing a little on them and manipulating them dexterously with his fingertips, could shuffle them around as nimbly as if they were a deck of cards. He was like an artist, too, in the way he mixed his alloys and obtained the tints and colors he wanted. He could create red, pale red, deep red, orange, lemon, and other tints, or what was simply called fine gold.

At the moment, Mr. Lundy was just finishing a first beating, and a first beating required a seventeen-pound hammer. Men working on construction, Brad knew, generally used an eight-pounder, and that always looked like a mighty big sledge.

He was a tall, skinny man with a puckered, generous face, and now, stripped to the waist, he looked like a sweating mummy. He had been swinging that hammer, Brad knew, for hours. He put the hammer down, and said wearily but happily, "Well, that's that. The shoder tomorrow."

The "shoder" was the second beating. "Well, I see you've brought the annual quilt, Bradley."

Almost before Brad knew it, he was drinking a mug of hot chocolate.

"That's honest chocolate," said Mr. Lundy. "Imported proper by the blessings of our Sovereign."

Suddenly, feeling warm and friendly from the drink, Brad said, "Mr. Lundy, will you give me a little information?"

"I don't have too much, as I've frequently noted in the past," answered Mr. Lundy. "But that's never kept me from talking before, so go ahead."

"You're a King George man?" said Brad.

"I have been called such."

Brad said, "What's wrong with the King, trying to put this stamp tax over on us against our will?"

It was the coming Stamp Act which went officially into force in a few days, on the first of November, which was fomenting all the anger and speeches.

"What's wrong with a stamp tax?" asked Mr. Lundy benignly. "They have had one in England for years."

"But this is America!"

"America, yes. But we're Englishmen, aren't we?"

"Why should we support England?"

"Whoa, whoa," said Mr. Lundy. "The money thus raised, from the colonies, will be spent right here for the benefit of the colonies. There has never been no other intention. For garrisons, for one thing, for protection agin those hungry French and Spaniards. I got something to tell you. They's men in England, mean and abominable, I'll grant some bad ones, who want to tax the breeches off us, just to be contemptible. But they is others, and I have a notion the King is included, that wants to go mighty, mighty easy on us. That *why* the stamp tax. A stamp tax is sometimes considered the least annoyin' of all taxes, because there's no collector knocking at your door with his staff. Things, you might say, is taxed at the source. And the rich is taxed equal to the poor."

Somehow, this didn't sound quite right. Mr. Lundy looked serious, but it didn't sound quite right.

The stamp tax was a revenue stamp that was to go on newspapers and all legal documents, any kind of a legal transaction whatever.

Brad said, "All right. I'd like to argue this a minute. Say I'm a New England captain of a cod fishing boat.

I sail to the Banks with my partner, and we come home with a good haul, sell the catch to a wholesaler, who jobs the fish out in parcels to retailers. Whew! Look at the taxes there. A tax on the clearance papers for the ship, a tax on the partnership, and taxes clear down to the last buyer. Americans all from beginning to end, but paying a British tax."

"What's wrong with that? It buys flints and powder and bayonets to protect American hearthstones, doesn't it?"

"That's taxation without representation!" said Brad. "Yes."

"And that doesn't turn your stomach?"

"Not mine. Because I believe in it. That's the kind of a monarchy I hold with. A king is a king. They've not only been doing it in England for seven hundred years, but they've been doing it deliberate. It proves their power, so they're desperate now. The truth is, they'll settle for any tax, no matter how small, just a token tax —if they can slap it on you without your permission."

"And you think that's proper?"

"Yes. And that's the very word I'd use, proper."

"Well, I don't," said Brad.

"Well, I do," said Mr. Lundy sadly. "Maybe my mamma and papa raised me wrong."

It was then they realized they had a visitor.

A man was standing just inside the door, humbly, shivering a little from the chill outside.

He was an elderly scarecrow of a man, with thick-lensed spectacles and a big, lumpy nose. His black jacket and knee breeches looked musty, almost like castoffs, his yarn hose were knotty and snarled, but his buckled shoes were expensive, neatly blackened, gleaming. In his hand he held a lighted link, that torch of tow and pitch which gentlemen nightwalkers carried for protection through darkened streets. All at once, Brad recognized him.

He was the old man Piggot had spoken to that day at the foot of Seely Street, on the deck of the *Abigail Edwards*. Piggot had said he had just arrived from Philadelphia; had he been around all the time since then? Brad wondered.

Mr. Lundy looked at the apparition politely, but with no other expression whatever.

"My name is John J. Kutchin, sirs," said the man in a low voice. "Where have I wandered?"

"You are in Sumatra Alley," said Brad. "Where are you headed for?"

"I thought I was in Hanover Square," said Mr. Kutchin weakly.

"Hanover Square is four long blocks northeast of here," said Brad. "What happened?"

Mr. Kutchin screwed up his face, as though he were trying to remember. "I was going through the Square, up in its darkest corner, by that row of counting houses, and this man came up from behind me and asked to light his pipe from my link. That's all I seem to recall."

"What did this man look like?" asked Mr. Lundy, trying to sound interested, but not interested in anything at all, apparently, but King George and gold leaf.

"I really couldn't say," answered Mr. Kutchin.

Suddenly, with a creepy feeling coming over him, Brad asked, "Was he an ugly-looking ape of a man with a garnet earring?" Somehow Boston seemed to fit into this picture.

"I really couldn't say," repeated Mr. Kutchin. "Gracious, my head aches!"

Slowly, Mr. Kutchin went through his pockets. "It seems to be gone. I had a long purple leather wallet. It seems to be gone, and the two pounds in it also."

So it wasn't Boston, Brad decided. Boston was an agent, not a footpad. This was just another robbery. Hanover Square, badly lighted, was full of robberies after dark.

Reluctantly, Mr. Lundy got to his feet. He shuffled over to the old man and gingerly touched the nape of his neck, just below the back of his time-stained tricorn hat. Mr. Kutchin recoiled and a spasm passed over his face.

"Hurts?" asked Mr. Lundy.

"Excruciating," said Mr. Kutchin.

"My guess is that you got sandbagged," said Mr. Lundy. "But I don't see any blood or bump."

"Where is the nearest doctor?" asked Mr. Kutchin.

"Up the street a short ways," said Mr. Lundy. "But this boy here is a doctor, or anyways studying to be one. Take a look at it, Brad."

Brad went to the old man, parted his queue at the back of his neck, and examined the scalp.

"I don't see anything," he said. "But an injury of that sort can be the worst kind. A bad fracture and concussion, could be. You might go for a couple of days even, and then fall down dead. No matter what Mr. Lundy says, I'm not a doctor. I'm just learning. Come with me. We'd better see Dr. Doddridge."

As Brad and the old man left, the old man turned and said, "Thank you for your sympathy, Mr.——er——?"

"Lundy," said the goldbeater. "Knowed scarcely anywhere but up and down this crooked little street. But knowed here for what I am, a rabid, arguin' King George man."

There was no need for him to bring that in, Brad thought. But that was like him, always flying his Union Jack and ready for a verbal broadside with anybody.

Mr. Kutchin appeared not to hear. He followed Brad into the cold street.

So that was what happened when a roaring royalist came face to face with a deep-dyed rebel, Brad thought. Nothing, nothing to notice.

For Mr. John J. Kutchin was a deep-dyed rebel; Brad was convinced of this. Or he wouldn't have been so much at home on the deck of the *Abigail Edwards* that afternoon, or in such intimate and conspiratorial conversation with Piggot there.

When they came into the wax workshop, they found Dr. Doddridge alone, crouched spraddle-legged at the hearth, laboring with bellows, trying to bring more heat-giving flame into the greenish oak logs there. He was muffled to the ears in a fuzzy wool traveler's shawl, and his breath in the cold air came out in little cloudy puffs. He got hastily to his feet and came forward hospitably to meet his visitor.

Impassively, Brad explained the situation.

"I rarely practice these days," said the doctor reluctantly. "But an emergency is an emergency. I'll take a look at it."

Mr. Kutchin beamed. For the moment, anyhow, the pain that had been so excruciating in Mr. Lundy's shop seemed forgotten.

"I had just purchased a packet of tea," said Mr.

Kutchin, "when it happened." Tea was golden these days, and much prized. "I have it here in my pocket. How about this? When you've made your examination we'll brew a pot, and sit and talk a little, and get to know each other better."

"That would be very kind of you," said Dr. Doddridge, his face showing pleasure. "Yes."

Mr. Kutchin, smiling at Brad, said, "Perhaps you had better follow Ben Franklin's advice and get to bed. Thank you for your courtesy. Good night and good bye, young sir."

Brad flinched. He was being dismissed.

Dr. Doddridge, looking distressed, said, "Stay awake. I'll save you a cup, and call you down when our guest has departed."

"Yes, indeed," said Mr. Kutchin vaguely.

Brad climbed the stairs toward his room. But on the landing, outside his door, he came to a decision, and mounted the ladder to the roof. There was much that had happened in the last twenty minutes that disturbed him greatly. It was urgent that he talk with Piggot, and immediately.

He crossed the roof, passed the chimneys and the pigeon cages, and descended Duquesne's rooftrap. He knocked at Piggot's door and Piggot answered and gestured him in. He did it with his thumb, in that careless way he used to do it in the old days, before all this had come up, and gave Brad that slow, lopsided smile; and Brad knew—no matter how it sometimes seemed—things were actually as they had always been.

They sat in their familiar customary places, Piggot on the edge of the crude bed, Brad on the chair along the wall. Cobwebs hung from the attic rafters above them, and the dormer window, now closed to the autumn chill, was a glazed panel of blackness against the night beyond. Brad said, "I hate to do it, but now I'm going to have to ask you a question or two you're maybe not going to want to answer."

"Try me," said Piggot, but looked suddenly wary.

"Remember when we were at the foot of Seely last month with your cart, and you were aboard the *Abigail Edwards* and spoke with a man there? What was his name?"

"I suppose you've got a good personal reason for asking that?"

"Why?"

"A personal reason is the only reason that will make me tell you the truth."

"It's not only personal, it's serious."

"His name is Haney."

"Just who is he?"

"He's the Philadelphia leader of the Sons of Liberty."

"When I met him tonight, he told me his name was Kutchin. Mr. John J. Kutchin."

One thing you had to admit about Piggot; nothing ever got him off balance.

Completely relaxed, he said, "A man in his business has got to go by other names now and then. How did you happen to meet him?"

Brad told him of the episode at the goldbeater's carefully, and in accurate detail. At last, he said, "What is he up to, here on Sumatra?"

"I don't know," said Piggot, and looked genuinely thoughtful.

"He told me a string of lies, and pretty cunning ones," said Brad. "At first I believed him, and then, too late, I realized he was just using me. Using me to get him into Dr. Doddridge's, where he is right now, to get him in, naturally, as a stranger."

"I don't see it," said Piggot.

"He came into Lundy's, maybe at first to ask directions to Dr. Doddridge's, or maybe he saw me through the window, and recognized me, and made up that story on the spur of the moment and came in."

"Recognized you?"

"One thing I've learned the past couple of months is that a lot of people I've never even heard of seem to know a lot about Sumatra Alley."

Piggot asked, "What makes you think the sandbagging was a lie?"

"The lighted link he had in his hand. He was so bad, according to him, that he didn't even know where he was. Yet a little before, he told us, he had been knocked out in Hanover Square. What happened to the link while that was happening? If he was hit that hard, he must have gone down. And the link went down, too, there on the ground. Did it go out, or just lie there burning? Afterwards, did he pick it up and light it, or even just pick it up, when he was in such a daze, like he claimed?"

"Either is possible," said Piggot. "But what does he want with Dr. Doddridge?"

"That's what I'm here for," said Brad somberly. "That's what I want to ask *you*. You're the one who knows about these things."

"Dr. Doddridge is neutral in all this," said Piggot. "Nobody could want anything with Dr. Doddridge."

"I know. That's what scares me. If it was Mr. Lundy he was interested in, I could understand it. Mr. Lundy's a fireball royalist."

"What do you mean by that?" asked Piggot.

"I was thinking of Boston. The rebels must have people like Boston on their side of the fence."

"I don't know," said Piggot. "And I'm glad I don't. But again, why Dr. Doddridge?"

"Could it be because Dr. Doddridge got Master Duquesne and me out of jail that time?"

"Mr. Haney is a rebel leader. Master Duquesne is a rebel. Mr. Haney would have done it himself, if he'd been here, and could have, and it had been a matter of choice with him."

"I don't mean that. I mean the way Dr. Doddridge did it. He did it through that ferocious royalist, Captain Lynnwood of the Georgia Rangers. And that meant Captain Lynnwood had to act through the King's Governor himself. King's Governor, Captain of the King's Georgia Rangers, and when you come right down to it, that's swinging around a lot of high-powered British authority for a man like Dr. Doddridge, who is, in fact, supposed to be absolutely neutral, like you said."

"But you said . . ." answered Piggot.

"I know what I said," declared Brad. "I said Captain Lynnwood did it because he wanted that plaque finished. That was what I was told. Now I wonder."

"And you think someone might have thought, 'We'll wait a little, and send Mr. Haney around and ask a few questions and find out a little more about this'?"

"That could be one of Mr. Haney's jobs. He could be a first-class questioner."

"If this is true," said Piggot, "the thing they wouldn't like is that maybe Dr. Doddridge is *pretending* to be neutral. When a man pretends, lots of times he's hiding something dangerous."

They sat there, looking unhappy, both of them, for Piggot, too, loved Dr. Doddridge.

"If this was so," said Piggot slowly, "would you have a different feeling toward him?"

"Never," said Brad wretchedly.

"That's the right answer," said Piggot. "Battle flags and cannon balls and stamp taxes and all that is mighty important, but that's the right answer."

Brad got up to leave.

Piggot said, "I don't know what those two men, Mr. Haney and Dr. Doddridge, are saying right now, but I can tell you one thing. The doctor's a deep one, with a mighty good tongue. I doubt if anyone, even Mr. Haney, will ever trap him with words."

When Brad got back, Dr. Doddridge was sitting in his bedroom on a stool, a crockery teapot on his knee, waiting for him. The doctor's face was placid, uncommunicative, amiable as usual. He said, "I brought your tea up for you. I judge you've got about twelve ounces of the delicious elixir here."

"Mr. John J. Kutchin gone?" asked Brad.

"Gone," said the doctor.

"He got in through a trick," said Brad. "I think that sandbagging story was a lie. I think he wanted to talk to you, and make the whole thing seem accidental."

"Is that so?" said Dr. Doddridge with a twinkle in his eye.

"What did he talk to you about?" asked Brad.

"Not very much, I'm afraid. Somehow I got off at

the start before he did. And found myself in that story of how I got that fishbone out of that little boy's throat back in London in the old days. That story has to be recounted in a lengthy manner, to do it justice. In fact, towards the end, I had to touch him several times on the shoulder to waken him while I was telling it."

"This is good tea," said Brad, relieved, drinking it from the broken teacup on his washstand.

"I thought so, too," said the doctor. "And it was absolutely free."

Brad met his steady gaze.

"And when I say absolutely," said the doctor, "I mean absolutely."

8

For some time Colonel James, the British gentleman-officer in charge of Fort George, the man who had said the tax stamps should be crammed down rebel throats with his sword, had been reinforcing the fort, preparing for the defense he expected—and Piggot had predicted—and on the night of November 1, it came. The fort was attacked.

This was the day the Stamp Act law went into effect.

And when the violence came, full force, no one in the town was greatly surprised. They were astounded at its magnitude, both British and American citizenry, but not actually surprised at its emergence.

Early in the day, in fact, much of that anti-British feeling, which had remained partly hidden all along, came out and displayed itself. There were processions in the streets, mock funerals to the death of Liberty. Crape was hung in taverns. Bells were tolled.

All day long, a feeling spread through the town, through streets and back streets and alleys, that big trouble would be the climax to all of this, and that when the trouble came, it would take place at the fort.

Brad asked permission to go and look, but the doctor refused.

"We've got our own troubles," he said. "We'll just stay here and leave well enough alone."

Very rarely did the doctor show any sternness whatever, and Brad showed his disappointment.

Softening a little, Dr. Doddridge said, "Doesn't your very instinct tell you to stay away?"

"My very instinct tells me to go."

So Brad stayed home that night in Sumatra Alley. But Piggot went. Piggot was there. Later, he told Brad all about it.

Master Duquesne was there, too.

Fort George, at the very southern tip of the city, had become, over the years, an enormous establishment, in area at least. Its rear, or town, side extended from Whitehall Street four blocks west, four blocks of stone wall and bastions and gates and cannonmouth, barring it from the town and the people of the town; to its south it followed the nose of the shoreline to the sea's edge, its walls here based on water-washed searock.

It looked what it was, a symbol and a mailed fist of the Empire. Over the years, it had for a time fallen into neglect and disrepair, but Colonel James had rectified that.

The spacious area within its walls housed not only the garrison and the armory, but the residence of the Governor, at the moment Lieutenant Governor Colden. Here, within the enclosure, were held the dazzling, fashionable social activities, as British as anything in London, and maybe a little more so.

The landward side, the town side, faced an open space between the fort and the town proper, and this space, from time immemorial, had served important public functions. In the days of early English rule, a market fair had been held there by royal order every Thursday, Friday, and Saturday. Later, when it was

used by the garrison for exercising, it became known
officially as The Parade. Thirty-some years ago, the
Corporation, in a resolution, had decided to "lease a
piece of land lying at the lower end of Broadway,
fronting the Fort to some of the inhabitants, in order to
be enclosed to make a Bowling-Green there, with walks
therein, for the beauty and ornament of said street, as
well as for the delight of the inhabitants of this
city."

It was here, at the landward side of the fort wall,
in this open space, that the assembly of hostile rebels
began. And having assembled, they moved forward to
the fort's main gate, facing and almost touching the
great cannon. They were three thousand strong.

None of the men of that small British garrison would
ever forget the hours until daybreak; nor would Lieutenant Governor Colden or brimstone-and-fire Colonel
James, for that matter.

And not once during those hours were the great fort
cannons served; never were their touchholes fired
in defense. The cannons would have slaughtered hundreds, of course. Later, the garrison's attitude was ex-
pressed on this point. If three thousand had been
killed that day, in two days twenty thousand others
would have confronted the British in horrendous re-
prisal.

This buzzing, shouting army was composed of
townsmen, sailors ashore, and others, armed only with
an anger that ranged from indignation to unleashed rage.

Milling, the crowd attempted to burn the fort. But
fortifications designed by British engineers, probably
the best in the world, were not to be demolished by a
rebellious citizenry. The fury continued. Pressed thick

as swarming bees, men beat upon the gate with cudgels and walking sticks. Lieutenant Governor Colden's elegant coach was discovered outside the walls, and was put to flames with boisterous laughter. Dawn was brightening the sky toward South Street before the last angry rebel melted away.

Later that morning, talking to Piggot in a hushed voice in a doorway on Sumatra, Brad said, "Well, they didn't take it and they didn't burn it."

"That's right," said Piggot, unworried.

"And the British didn't even fire their cannons."

"And wisely."

"So what did we gain?" asked Brad.

"Wait and see," said Piggot.

Brad waited as Piggot had advised, and soon he saw.

Some two weeks later, Governor Moore showed up and replaced Lieutenant Governor Colden. The city, to the quickly scanning eye at least, seemed to come back to reasonably good order. But never again outside the fort, within the city proper, was British military authority anything but a halfhearted empty gesture.

There were those who even had a good word to say for Governor Moore.

Among other things, he declined to execute the Stamp Act.

9

Now the great drowsy bear which was the thirteen colonies, having in the past shown its claws a few times in its half-slumber, rolled upright to its haunches and showed its teeth. From Maine to Florida, defiance to Crown and Empire became more and more open and ominous. And another element had entered the picture. Now united with the Liberty Boys were not only seamen, but their captains; not only counting-house clerks, but their masters; not only dockhands and warehousemen, but owners and merchant princes. This was incredible to the leaders in London, who in the past had deceived themselves too easily in believing that the rebels were simply restless troublemaking riffraff, by and large. There had been a few exceptions, yes, but now rebellion became popular, and in places it became fashionable. In New York, a small group of dim-witted hoity-toity beaux organized their own Sons of Liberty and tried to make an exclusive high-society dance, dine and strutting-promenade thing out of it. But soon they lost interest in such weighty matters as freedom and independence and representation, and went back to arguing about how high a stock should be and the proper lace to wear at one's wrists.

Other Sons of Liberty, the genuine article, were discussing and arguing, too, but without public notice, meeting in secret conclaves in the Carolinas and Mary-

88

land, and especially Massachusetts, and elsewhere. And among the subjects discussed by these men were knappers of gunflints, and the price of French bayonets per thousand, and the location of British powder magazines.

Brad, excited like everyone else, dreading and yet hoping, tried one morning at breakfast to get some answers from Dr. Doddridge. But Dr. Doddridge wasn't too helpful. Of all the people Brad knew, the doctor was the only one who seemed unaware and completely uninterested in the events that were bursting around him. He lived in America, true. And in New York City, true. And on Sumatra Alley, true. But in form only. In reality, he existed in one place only, it seemed to Brad: in that busy cranium of his, enclosed in that big imposing skull.

Brad, disregarding all table manners, placed a fried egg and two rashers of bacon sprinkled with sage between two thick, buttered cornmeal pancakes, making a voluptuous sort of sandwich. Cutting it with care, he stowed a bale-sized portion in his mouth and, chewing slowly, said, "Well, then, let me put it this way. Are things good or bad? You certainly must have an opinion on that!"

"Who can say?" answered the doctor, eating his simple monastic meal of unsweetened coffee and unbuttered bread. "Good or bad? To Mr. Lundy, the loyal King's man, they must seem bad. To Mr. Huggins, just across the narrow street from him, Mr. Huggins who has so many children with measureless appetites and sees so much import-export money going directly across the sea to England, into silk-lined English pockets, any change must seem good."

"Silk-lined," said Brad. "Now, for the first time I've caught you. For the first time I've fathomed how your deep feelings really run. You're pro-American, I'm glad to say. You could have just said pockets, English pockets. You put in the silk-lined because you don't like those pockets!"

Dr. Doddridge showed his teeth happily in soundless laughter. "Those are your words, not mine," he said. "Don't ride that horse too far and too fast; it might throw you on your ear."

A little later in the morning, when Brad had a few minutes' spare time, he decided to drop in and have a little easy, oblique conversation with Mr. Huggins. Time and again, since that talk with Boston at the sign of the Anchor Smith in Queen's Court, Brad had thought about Mr. Huggins. At first it had seemed absurd that Mr. Huggins could be a center of interest for a British agent. But whose name had popped into Dr. Doddridge's mouth when he had been trying to select a typical rebel at breakfast? Why, Mr. Huggins'!

Brad decided he would drop in, talk a little, and sound him out. If he thought it at all possible that Mr. Huggins could fit the picture, he would warn him. If, after he had sounded him out, he decided to his own satisfaction that he didn't fit the picture, that Boston couldn't possibly be after him, then Brad would merely trail it off into a friendly visit and say nothing.

When Brad entered the harpsichord maker's shop, Mr. Huggins was pulling a troublesome baby tooth from one of his younger children. He was doing it with a pair of sharp-pointed harpsichord-wire pliers, which he had dipped in honey first, hoping this would distract the child during the operation. It didn't. The child was yelling his head off. Mr. Huggins, seeing Brad, said, "I don't mind the yelling. I'm used to it. But he keeps jerking his body."

Brad said, "Why don't you tighten him up in that big woodworker's vise? That would steady him."

"I don't think that's funny," said Mr. Huggins, and Brad could tell he didn't.

"I'm sorry," said Brad.

And now Mr. Huggins' gentle, sympathetic nature went immediately to Brad. He said, "I know. Forget it."

All at once it became impossible to believe that a man like Mr. Huggins, who so adored his family, who so loved his domesticity, would place everything in jeopardy by conspiring against established law and order, against the sanctity of the Crown, a conspiracy so profound and critical that it would be marked by officialdom for extinction and bring a man like Boston on his trail. Just standing there, watching Mr. Huggins fussing and cooing over his little boy, Brad knew in his bones he couldn't be the one.

Nevertheless, Brad tried a clincher. He said, "I consider you a friend. I need some advice. Important and personal."

Without turning around, Mr. Huggins said, "What's wrong with Dr. Doddridge? He's a wiser specimen than I."

"It's the nature of the advice," said Brad.

At that moment, Mr. Huggins extracted the tooth. He put down his pliers, faced Brad, and said quietly, "Let's have it."

This was a different Mr. Huggins, self-assured, rock hard, competent. Respect and surprise surged through Brad like a hot flame. He hated to go on with his little fiction, but he did. It was for Mr. Huggins' safety; he had to look at it that way. He said, "Like most peo-

ple these days, I guess, I've been thinking about linking
up with the Independence movement. That's it. What
should I do?"

"You'll have to work that one out yourself," said Mr.
Huggins. "It's a matter of conscience."

"But I thought you'd say, 'Join,'" said Brad. "I
thought you were anti-British."

"I'm anti-tyranny, but pro-British," said Mr. Huggins.
"If I'm anything."

"But Dr. Doddridge said otherwise."

"Many people jump to hasty conclusions about me,"
said Mr. Huggins. "Frequently I fail to make myself
clear. I'm not against the King, against the Parliament,
against the Government. I'm just against some of the
unfortunate decisions those august bodies put into law.
I'm in favor of law itself, though, aren't you?"

"Why, naturally."

"Then I'm afraid you're pretty much like I am. For
a British national, it's British law. You are a British national, aren't you?"

Brad set his jaw and made no answer.

"Think these matters out," said Mr. Huggins placidly. "Now I must get back to my carving. I will hold
this little conversation in confidence, and expect you
to do the same."

"Yes, sir," said Brad. "I will."

It was a low-down way to find out things, but Brad
felt this man had spoken from his heart to him.

He was in good spirits as he left the shop. Mr. Huggins and his family were in no danger. Boston's target
was otherwise.

Outside, he started for Master Duquesne's confectionery and a talk with Piggot.

Up the cobbles, in front of his own shop, stood a wretched little blacker boy, rags and grime and tatters, his crude, homemade shoeshine box on the stones by his ankle. He was staring at Dr. Doddridge's front door. He was a stranger in a strange land here, for the denizens of Sumatra Alley were more interested in the flexibility of their fingers than in the gloss on their boots.

Brad gave the boy a hard look as he turned into Master Duquesne's. Ever since he had been a street boy himself, he always gave blacker boys a careful scrutiny. They might look cherubic, they might talk with a charming little chirping, they might be able to wail and turn their tears on and off in torrents, but they lived a life of crime in a world of crime that would whiten a watchman's hair. They weren't footpads (too small to swing a lead-weighted bludgeon), or highwaymen (too small to gallop a horse), but many of them, working with older men, were already veteran pickpockets and house breakers.

Well, if he was considering the pickpocket lay, or the housebreaking lay, for that matter, on Sumatra he was really wasting his time.

When Brad came in, Master Duquesne was rushing around as usual, this time concocting a spice brine for pickling walnuts. Here was the man, Brad thought, who could, perhaps, answer many of the little problems that bothered him, but the answers would be multiple and long-winded and half of them would be sure to contradict and conflict with the other half, and when you got through listening to him, you wouldn't know anything at all.

Master Duquesne nodded genially to Brad. Brad

nodded in response, passed him, and entered the storeroom.

Piggot, who had piled out of bed in the predawn so ovens could be heated and tarts cooked and drawn and delivered in time for gentlefolks' breakfasts, was having his first real meal of the day, a bowl of rice mixed with chopped corned beef and crumbled hard-boiled egg.

Brad sat beside him on the wooden bench and said, "It looks like you've finally got your wagon rolling downhill, all right, no brakes. When is it going to get to uniforms and muskets?"

"Have some rice and beef?" Piggot asked.

"Well, when?"

"Don't ask me. I'm nobody."

"Well, it's here, you can't get around that, and I'm glad," said Brad.

Piggot ate in silence.

Moodily, Brad said, "I wouldn't have believed it. Everybody, almost. And it came all at once—"

"No. Not all at once."

"Well, it seemed to come all at once. It was the attack on Fort George that did it, wasn't it?"

"No, it wasn't Fort George," said Piggot. "Fort George pushed it along a little, but it wasn't Fort George."

"Then what was it?"

"Like you mighty well know, it goes back, way back. To each and every one of the thirteen colonies."

"They had more than they could stomach."

"They had more than they could stomach, but there's a heap more to it than that. Each of these colonies had a big complaint with England, but each had a bigger complaint, or so they thought, with some of their neighbor colonies. North with south, inland with seacoast, planters with merchants, prosperous with unprosperous, ignorant with wise, husbands with wives, dogs with cats, everything with everything. My, my, my!"

Brad smiled. "I know."

"So someone had to come along who could help them separate the wheat from the chaff. Someone who could show them all how to pull together."

"Men like Otis and Hancock up in Boston?"

"Like them, surely. But it could be, just possibly could be, that a lot of this isn't being handled from Boston—but here in New York City."

"You mean from the *Abigail Edwards?*"

"I don't know for sure. If the British don't know, how could I know?"

"Well, guess. What's wrong with a guess?"

They stared at each other. The thought of the growing rebellion glowed in their eyes.

After a long, long moment of silence, Piggot said thinly, "Then I'll guess right here from the confectionery. I'll guess Master Duquesne."

Brad refused to take this seriously. "But the British have already had him in their jail and released him. I like Master Duquesne, but he's all glittering eyes and flashing teeth, and mixed-up talk."

"Is that so?" said Piggot. "Then you know him better than I do."

When Brad stepped out of the confectionery into the street, a heavy gray sky, dull and lightless, had lowered itself to just above the chimneytops, it seemed, and visibility was clouded by a veil of huge

snowflakes so muffling and wet that they seemed not
to drift down but to drop.

The urchin with his shoeshine box was standing,
waiting. He screwed his face into a fawning whine,
the one all blacker boys put on for strangers, and
asked, "Where can I find Brad Agnew?"

"You've found him," said Brad suspiciously.
"You're talking to him."

The urchin pointed. "There's a hackney coach at
the end of the street, reined up for you."

"I want no coach," said Brad curtly. "I've hired
no coach."

"When you come right down to it," said the boy,
"you don't know whether you want it or not. Why
don't you go and see? The driver sent me to say
this."

Any hackney driver, even under the most favor-
able conditions, was an animal to beware of. They
and their kind were the dregs of dregs. With all of
them, almost without exception, it was a part-time,
hit-or-miss profession. What they did at other times,
it was known, might well be done at midnight with
a brace of pistols on a lonely common, or with a
center bit and a burglar's ivory gag among the plate
and table silver in the residence of a wealthy merchant. Find the lowest alehouse, sullen with bawds
and ruffians, and you would find among them hackney
coachmen indistinguishable and at home.

"I've no time for such," said Brad shortly.

"In that case I am to mention a name to you. Mr.
John J. Kutchin, at times known by his real name,
Haney."

The rebel leader from Philadelphia.

"Is he in the coach?" asked Brad.

But the urchin was gone.

Brad turned and walked slowly through the snow in the direction that had been indicated to him.

He was quite sure he was doing the right thing.

10

At the corner, when the coach loomed up suddenly before him out of the snow, it seemed to be just an ordinary hackney coach, two horses, inside capacity for eight. The horses were a little sway-backed, and the driver, leaning down from his high seat, muffled, warty-faced, villainous-looking, could have been a little more shipshape, but there was nothing to be alarmed about. What alarmed Brad was that the coach was empty of passengers.

He came to a stop, his hand already on the door handle, and said, "You're empty. Where's the gentleman?"

"Git in," said the driver.

"You were supposed to have a passenger. I was told to—"

"You was told to come here, and that only. Git in."

"Not likely," said Brad. "What's going on?"

"Was the name 'Mr. John J. Kutchin' passed on to you?"

"Yes," said Brad warily.

"Then my duty is done and finished," said the driver. "The rest, I was informed, would be up to you. I've been paid whether you come or not. What's it to be?"

"I'm coming," said Brad, changing his mind. He got in.

Eight minutes later he wondered if he had made the wrong decision, for the coach was bumping down Wales Street, in one of the most festering sections of the city.

On either side of the frozen, rutted street was a string of hovels, low-eaved affairs of odds and ends, each with its pig pen of planks behind or perhaps at its side along the walk. There were cold, unhappy chickens on doorsteps, and bawling goats, too. The chill, humid air was oppressive with the odor of rotting garbage, pigs' food. No humans were in sight, and the snow, fluffy and deepening by now, showed not a single track of boot or shoe—man, woman, or child. These, Brad knew, would be people who preferred to crawl from their closed doors only at night, after early candlelight. They would live by pilfering, by rolling artificial flowers, by doing laundry at home, and by rifling dustbins. Those of them who emerged by day subsisted by collecting and dealing in bones, catskins, broken crockery, and rags.

The coach ground to a stop. The driver pointed to a front door and said, "There."

Brad got out. The coach rumbled away.

An old woman with a short clay pipe clenched in her gapped teeth answered his knock on the door. She looked him over and said, "Yes, young master?"

Young master. Brad smiled. Dr. Doddridge always saw that he dressed right. Proper clothes, proper speech, and proper general deportment, the doctor kept saying, would be important to a coming physician.

"I want to see Mr. Haney," said Brad.

"Is that his name?" she said.

"You don't know?"

"Why should I? He's just my lodger. Lots of lodgers, I've learned, don't seem to have any names at all."

She stepped back and Brad found himself in a bare, cold room; he could hardly tell the difference from outside in the snow. With her pipestem she pointed across the room to a closed door.

Brad followed the direction indicated and rapped. A muffled voice called, "Come in."

Brad entered.

This room was nice and warm. A roaring, fluttering fire burned in its small fireplace. There was a sawed-down corded bed in one corner, covers helter-skelter, several broken-down chairs, crudely mended, and a table with the remnants of a meal on it, a little mound of rabbit bones (rabbit or cat, you never knew for sure in this kind of neighborhood), and a heel of bread. Behind the table sat a man, grinning at him.

The man, garnet earring, ape shoulders, wet, puffy lips and all, was Boston Hollingsworth.

"This time I've got you," he said.

Brad said nothing.

"Got you dead to rights," said Boston.

Brad simply looked at him.

"From now on," said Boston, "you're my little King Charles spaniel. You belong to me body and soul. When I snap my fingers, you come crawling. When I kick you, you go."

"What do you mean?" said Brad, feeling a touch of dread at the man's bullying confidence.

"I've jest give you a little test, with interestin' results," said Boston.

Brad merely stared. He knew the test all right, knew how firmly he had been trapped.

Boston said slowly, enjoying himself, "I had you figgered as nobody, jest an innocent young whipper-snapper who by accident happened to be living in a nest of rebels, yonder over on Sumatra. Who did you come here to see?"

"I've got to leave," said Brad. "I'm needed back at the shop."

"A name brought you here. And the name was Mr. Kutchin-Haney, the big rebel leader who comes here sometimes, and always stays on the *Abigail Edwards*. The *Abigail Edwards* and Haney of Philadelphia, and you puttin' yourself off to me as jest a harmless young feller that don't know nothing about nothing."

The explanation to all this was so complicated that Brad didn't even start to tackle it.

Between flattened lips, Boston said, "The man we want, the man I told you about is still doing business on Sumatra. When you leave here, you're going to nose him out for me."

"We've talked about this before," said Brad.

"But never this way. I don't like to be gulled."

"I don't expect you to believe me," said Brad. "But I don't have any idea—"

"You're going to dig up an idea. That's the point. You're going to find out. Or—"

"Or what?" said Brad.

"Or you're going to sea," said Boston, and Brad could tell from the way he said it that he meant it, really meant it.

"Oh, no, I'm not," said Brad quietly.

"Oh, yes, you are," said Boston just as quietly.

"Here's what's going to happen. You'll be walking along some street some day, or night, for that matter, and the next thing you know you'll wake up in the scuppers of some ship, a seaman headed on a long voyage."

"Who is going to do it?" said Brad, knowing that it had been done hundreds and hundreds of times.

"I'm going to do it personal, mayhap. Say, helped by the very hackney driver that brought you here. Nobody can do nothing, because you'll be gone without a trace. And it won't cost me a penny. In fact, me and my friend will turn a little profit, because we'll *sell* you to the ship's mate."

The fire in the fireplace spluttered and coughed and blazed.

"It'll kill you, o' course," said Boston in a matter-of-fact tone.

"I doubt it," said Brad, putting up a faint bluff. "I may like it. I may thrive on it. Other boys have gone to sea and it hasn't killed them."

"I'll pick a ship that *will* kill you. That kills with overwork, and replaces. That makes a practice of such. Do you know what pickling is?"

Boston expected no answer, got none, and went on. "Pickling is being stretched up to the mast and flogged. The pickling comes afterward. Your split back is then rubbed with salt. Some captains prefers salt and vinegar, mixed."

Now Brad's fear had passed. He knew the man was speaking the truth, but how did being scared help any? He said levelly, "I have a feeling that you yourself will die at somebody's yardarm."

"Likely, very likely," said Boston contentedly. "But

that won't be no help to you, will it? But along with all
this, I'm going to do you a favor."

"I bet."

"I'm going to send a friend along with you. A
friend. Your special friend. Duquesne's boy, Piggot.
We may not pick the two of you up at the same time,
probably not, but close enough together to place you
on the same deck, for the same voyage."

"Keep Piggot out of this," said Brad through
parched lips.

"You're the only one can keep him out," said Boston. "Now clear out. Get along."

Though it was only a little after noon when Brad
got back to Sumatra, the low-hanging storm sky had
darkened the narrow, crooked street almost to dusk.
Wet, frothy snow layered the window ledges, and
puffs and clots of it stood up on the cobbles like cot-
ton. Where the inside heat of buildings had melted
it, stone and brick and iron railings gleamed moistly.
The whale-oil lamps were lighted in shops, and but-
tery-yellow light glowed faintly through windowpanes.
When Brad came to the shop of Mr. Lundy, the goldbeater, he turned in. He was late coming home already, and he might as well be a little later, he decided.

He had to talk Boston Hollingsworth over with someone, and Mr. Lundy, if you could keep him off his
rabid loyalty for the King and Empire, was as level-
headed as anyone Brad knew. He didn't want to con-
sult Dr. Doddridge on the point, because the doctor
would get so angry that it would confuse him, and he
discarded Piggot for the same general reason.

When Brad came into the goldbeater's shop, clos-

ing the door carefully behind him, closing out the snow
and wind and almost the memory of Boston, he saw
Mr. Lundy had a visitor, and, of all people, it was
Master Duquesne. They were sitting easily, chatting
sociably, as relaxed as friends, as old and close friends,
in fact. Boisterous rebel and boisterous King's man.
Brad blinked at the scene. If they were close friends,
this was the first time since he had lived on Sumatra
that he had received the slightest indication of it.

When they saw Brad, their manner changed and
they put on a pretense of being brisk and business-
like with each other.

Master Duquesne got to his feet. He said, "So you
wouldn't advise my putting a gold-leaf sign on my
shop door?"

Mr. Lundy said, "You don't need it. You don't
retail there, and you've got a city-wide reputation of
the best sort. If you want gold leaf, I can sell it to
you, of course, but it would be an entirely unneces-
sary expense."

"Thank you," said Duquesne, and then, as he
passed Brad, he said, "Hello, Brad."

When Master Duquesne had gone, Mr. Lundy said,
"What's happened to you? Look at those sopping
feet."

"I've just walked back from Wales Street," said
Brad.

"Well, you better get home and dry them out. Dry
them slow, and afterwards rub them with a little
lamb fat, to soften them out and make them look
better."

"Where I might be going, I probably won't even be

wearing shoes most of the time. I'll probably be going barefoot like the others."

Shooting up one eyebrow and pulling down a corner of his lips, Mr. Lundy said, "What's this? What are you talking about? Just where are you going?"

"It could be anyplace. Java maybe, or China, or Sooloo. I could even wind up on a terrible slaver to the Ivory Coast."

Sardonically, Mr. Lundy said, "As I understand it, you're not bound by contract to Dr. Doddridge, just sort of a gentleman's agreement. So I guess you could go, if your head's set on it."

"My head isn't set on it," exclaimed Brad. "It's set just the opposite! That's what I want your advice on."

Brad told him all about Boston. How he and Piggot had first met him that night in Piggot's attic bedroom. How later, when Brad and Master Duquesne had been arrested, Boston had been on hand, and Boston had tried to trick him into escaping jail. He told him about the talk he had had with Boston at the sign of the Anchor Smith that day.

Then, taking a big breath, he told him about the incident he had just gone through. This was the bad part, for it involved mentioning Mr. Haney of Philadelphia.

Mr. Lundy listened placidly. When Brad had finished, he said, "Knowing my background and my political opinions, you tell me this? Why?"

"Because, somehow, I consider you a friend. Because I'm in need of advice. And I know whatever I tell you now, you'll just put in a little pocket of your brain and forget. You're a wild crazy royalist, but

I have a feeling in my bones that first of all you're a man of honor."

The rims of Mr. Lundy's eyes suddenly went fiery red. There were no tears, but Brad got an idea somehow that the man was mighty close to crying.

When he spoke, though, his voice was so low it seemed almost docile. "Thank you, Brad. I only hope I'm half the man, or half as honorable, as you've just showed yourself."

"So what should I do?" asked Brad.

"That's a pretty hard question to answer," said Mr. Lundy. "First I'd say I ought to go around to Wales Street when you've told me how to locate the place, and have a little chat with him. And I'll take along my seventeen-pound hammer, in case I should want to knock a fly off anyone's head."

"No," said Brad, not wanting to drag Mr. Lundy into this. "Please don't." His mind, whizzing, began to try to think of reasonable objections. "He'll probably be gone. It was just a private home and one of those places where lodgers come and go, I'd say. The woman there, she said she didn't even know the names of a lot of them."

"You may be right," said Mr. Lundy reluctantly.

"So we're right back where we started," said Brad. "What shall I do?"

"I don't know," said Mr. Lundy. "I've got to tell you the truth. I don't know."

"I guess I'll just have to face it," said Brad with a stiff, dry smile.

"I could tell you to stay out of dark passageways, and always keep a sharp lookout, and things like that," said Mr. Lundy. "But I refuse to degrade this fine conversation with such pompous trivialities."

As Brad nodded and started for the door, Mr. Lundy, behind him, said, "But I can tell you this. If anything happens to you, I shouldn't be surprised if Piggot, Dr. Doddridge, Duquesne, Mr. Huggins, and myself searched out this Boston, and found him wherever he might be. And shook a stern finger under his nose."

The mildness with which Mr. Lundy spoke gave Brad goose pimples.

Mr. Lundy said, "But that doesn't seem to be the right answer, does it?"

"No. I'm afraid not, sir."

"It wouldn't be to me, either," said Mr. Lundy regretfully. "And of course it isn't, but it's the best I can do."

Brad left the shop and went out into the street. Piggot wouldn't even be with them. Piggot would be with him, Brad.

The snow had stopped and a great wet silence filled the world. Little paw tracks, dogs', cats', had punched the feathery white blanket. For them, at least, things were pretty much back to usual.

They had no Boston in their lives.

11

"Well, Tapscott's got his toothache back again," said Dr. Doddridge as Brad came out of the little chimney-corner doorway next morning and seated himself at a steaming bowl of mush and honey and thick cream.

Brad, who had never heard of any Tapscott, picked up his spoon and said, "Who is he?"

"Marjoribanks Tapscott, Esquire," said Dr. Doddridge dreamily. "Certainly you've heard me mention him."

"Not that I recall," said Brad politely.

"I knew him years ago when we were young together in London, and more or less consistently ever since. He gets these thunder-and-lightning skull-splitting toothaches and won't let anyone minister to them but me. And I'm not even a dentist, but a physician. It knocked Taps out of bed this morning, I understand. Well, we'll have to take care of him."

Brad wondered how the doctor had got the word so quickly, but asked no questions.

The doctor held up a phial partly filled with liquid. "Laudanum," he said. "I'd appreciate it if you'd take it to him. He knows the proper dosage."

"Be glad to," said Brad.

The doctor left the room. When he returned, the

bottle was wrapped in a twist of paper. "I'd like the bottle back," he said. "He can transfer it to a bottle of his own. And accept no fee, please."

"Where do I take it?" asked Brad.

"Let me think," said the doctor, frowning. "Is it the Queen's Head, near the Exchange? No. Is it the Golden Hill? No. The Province Arms? No. Now I remember. It's the King's Arms. On Broadway between Crown and Little Prince Streets."

These hostelries were all feverishly British, and the King's Arms was the most notorious of the lot. It was the favorite resort of officers from Fort George, social, expensive, fashionably rakehell. Lord Cornbury had once ridden his horse through its door up to the bar and elegantly requested a drink.

"Yes, sir," said Brad, getting up.

"And the bottle comes back," said the doctor. "Don't forget, bottle back."

"Yes, sir," said Brad. "I'll remember."

"One thing more," said the doctor. "You could ask for Henshaw. He's a servant there."

The doctor could not at first remember the name of the inn, but had no trouble remembering the name of one of its servants.

"Why not just ask for Mr. Tapscott himself?" said Brad. "That's the way I'd do it. You wouldn't want a bottle of laudanum floating around in careless hands."

"Suit yourself," said the doctor agreeably. "I was just trying to make it quicker for you. You'll see it's quite an establishment."

Walking leisurely west, Brad hit Broadway at its lower end and turned north. This, the lower end of

Broadway, was the city's most fashionable neighborhood, having as its only near rival Pearl Street. Here
were mansions of the Governor, and the collector of the
port, among other fabulously wealthy persons. The
tree-lined stretch reaching north as far as Trinity
Church had become known as the Mall. The dwelling
houses were all magnificent, and many of the lots on
the west side of Broadway, though averaging but fifty
feet in width, extended back to the Hudson.

Little Prince Street was four blocks north, just beyond the last of the great residences.

The King's Arms was an old gray house, with mis-
matched. mismated windows. It had a cupola, empty
now but in summer supplied with tables and seats and
a telescope, so that gentlemen so inclined could view
the Hudson with their repast. Along the street, in front
of the building, extending north and south for some
distance, were catalpa trees, bleak and clawlike today
in the dreary winter morning, but lush with perfumed
blooms on a balmy spring day. Before the inn's door was
its swinging sign, depicting the lion and the unicorn
fighting for the crown.

There was nothing in London to surpass its British
charm.

A menial on the doorstep glared at Brad as he entered the parlor.

To the rear, Brad could see the dazzling barroom,
with its little cubbyholes screened with green Chinese
silk, for customers who wished privacy. To one side of
the barroom, he could see a section of the large
dining room. Though it was scarcely ten in the morning, the place was crowded with British officers, hand-
some and straight in their crisp and beautiful—but
hated—uniforms. And as usual with British officers away

from their ranks, they gave off a merry atmosphere
of holiday. Here, in the parlor, there was no servant
or host in sight. Brad walked to the rear, passed
through the barroom, glancing about him, curious, and
stepped into the dining room.

British breakfasts were being served, breakfasts
which to Brad would have been sumptuous dinners:
mutton, veal, chicken, meat and fowl and fish of every
variety, served in every possible manner hot and cold
—chops, roasts, pies; and more custards and tarts and
breads than you could count. There were oysters
cooked in a little roll of bacon, lobsters in heavy cream
sauce with minced green and red peppers from the
Spanish Main.

There were servants here, plenty of them, almost
dancing in their eagerness to serve, all obsequious
and groveling—all except a man in a small-striped
apron, who was carrying a yellow lacquered table.
Brad gravitated toward him.

There was something about this Tapscott business
that Brad didn't like too much. On his walk here to
the King's Arms, he had decided he would like a
look at the man, if he could manage it, before he delivered the laudanum.

Brad said, "I know you're busy, and I hate to inter-
rupt you, but is Mr. Tapscott in the dining room?
Could you point him out?"

The man came to a halt, put the little yellow table
on the floor between them, by his knees, and said not
unkindly, "You want to break in on him while he's
eating, is that it?"

"I doubt if he's eating," said Brad. "He's half crazy
with a toothache."

"He's not here in the dining room," said the man,

lifting the table. "He's in his room, and you couldn't get in *there* with a three-brigade escort."

When Brad hesitated, and set his jaw, the man said firmly, "I mean it. What did you want with him, son?"

"Then direct me to another man," said Brad. "A man named Henshaw."

"I'm Henshaw," said the man cautiously.

Brad handed him the bottle and told his story.

"Wait outside," said Henshaw, and continued on his way.

About ten minutes later, as he stood outside under a catalpa tree, Brad was rejoined by the man in the striped apron, Henshaw.

"Here's the empty bottle," said Henshaw, handing it to him again wrapped in paper, accompanied by a coin. "And a shilling for your trouble, Mr. Tapscott says."

Brad remembered now that he had even forgotten to ask for the return of the bottle.

He took the bottle, but wouldn't touch the coin. "I was told to accept no money, and I think that meant no money at all," he said.

"Now that's exactly correct," said Henshaw, looking pleased and satisfied. "Sign and countersign. Good day and good luck to you."

And now he was gone. Back inside the tavern. Before Brad could answer.

Sign and countersign.

A block away, worried, Brad held the bottle up and looked at it. For one thing, it was wrapped in a different paper, a paper that looked almost the same but wasn't. He unwrapped it.

It was the same bottle all right, empty now, but there

was barely legible writing on the inside of the paper. It said:

> Captain Hayes of the Duke of Broking's Grenadiers reports to me to pass along to you the information that he has it on not too good authority that a goldbeater on your street, a Mr. Lundy, is suspect as the Royalist he makes out to be. We would like to know more about this.

He wrapped the bottle back up, and twisted the paper, carefully.

Piggot was vigorously sweeping off Master Duquesne's doorstep as Brad came up Sumatra.

Stopping before him, Brad said, "Can I trust you all the way?"

Piggot, sensing Brad's distress, leaned on his broom handle. His eyes went flinty dull. He said quietly, "I don't like that kind of a remark, coming from you. If you can't, who can?"

Brad told him about the errand he had just completed. He started to unwrap the bottle, but Piggot backed away.

"I want none of it," he said.

Numb, Brad stood and stared at him.

"You asked if you could trust me," said Piggot. "You can. I'll tell nobody."

He turned and went inside.

At the shop, Dr. Doddridge welcomed Brad, beaming. He said, "Thank you. How about a little lesson? Where are we now? Anodynes and antispasmodics?"

"We had them eight months ago," said Brad. "No lesson today, please. I don't feel too well."

Dr. Doddridge said nothing. Ordinarily, he would

have asked questions, made a diagnosis, and prepared something therapeutic.

Carelessly, he laid the bottle on the table.

Hardly an instant later, though, when Brad glanced that way, it was gone.

The doctor was gone, too.

That night, after supper, Brad paid a visit to Piggot in his attic bedroom. Brad, knowing from past experience how cold the room could be, wore his mittens and an old, knotty yarn muffler. Piggot, who seemed to have nothing but sinews and rawhide on that skinny skeleton of his and never seemed to notice cold, sat on a chair in a corner and said, "Well, on my own, I took a little journey over to the King's Arms after I talked with you and asked a few questions of a friend I have there. Careful questions, of course."

"Did you learn anything?" Brad asked.

"I learned that no one named Tapscott stays there, or has ever stayed there in anybody's memory. I don't think Marjoribanks Tapscott, Esquire, is anything more than a password between Dr. Doddridge and his friend Henshaw."

"I don't either," said Brad.

"My! There's sure a lot of British officers at the King's Arms," said Piggot. "Maybe now that the Liberty Boys have had their say about Fort George, they'll put the King's Arms next on their list. Is Dr. Doddridge at home tonight?"

Brad didn't want to discuss Dr. Doddridge, but he had no choice.

"Not tonight," said Brad. "He's taken a quilt around to Mr. Lundy."

"Lending him another? A second one?"

"He thinks it might be a cold winter, he told me," said Brad.

"Or a hot one," said Piggot.

12

That was Tuesday. In the next two days, Brad learned something. He learned that ties as strong as the ties between himself and the doctor couldn't be easily dissolved. Things went along as usual. He found himself feeling the same toward the doctor, and was pretty certain, all things considered, the doctor felt the same toward him. He was certain, though, that the doctor knew he had read the note, and there were moments when this seemed to sort of solidify between them and, without any words being spoken, embarrass each of them.

Late Thursday afternoon, when the western sky was tinted a soft rose madder, which promised a severe freezing for the night, and tiny golden stars overhead were blinking, lonesome and sparse, through the misty smoke from the chimney pots, Piggot showed him the orange peel.

They were standing by the doctor's shop, their backs against the front wall, not talking much, just comfortable and secure in each other's presence. They had just finished early supper.

All at once, Piggot took something from his jacket pocket and held it out in the palm of his hand for Brad's inspection.

"An orange peel," said Brad. "Well, what about it? You mean it's something special?"

"I think so," said Piggot.

Brad peered. "You mean is it a Valencia or a Portuguese one?"

"I mean, Where did I find it?"

"You could have found it anywhere," said Brad. "They're not common, but they're not rare, either."

"I found it in the cheese shop," said Piggot.

"What were you doing in the cheese shop?" asked Brad, interested more in this than in the orange peel. "And how did you get in?"

Next door to Duquesne's was the only empty shop on the street. Once it had been a cheese shop, but the owner had died and the heirs had boarded it up and forgotten it.

"I got in through the rooftrap," said Piggot. "Master Duquesne says one of these days I'm going to have to get rid of my rabbit and its hutch. He says rabbit hutches and confections don't mix. Well, I thought, nobody is using the shop next door. So I went down into it and looked it over. That's when I found it."

Unimpressed, Brad said, "What of it?"

Piggot amplified. "After a bit, orange peels get hard, mighty hard. This orange peel is still soft. It's fresh. I'd say hardly a couple of days old. Who has been in that shop in the last couple of days, taking it easy, eating an orange?"

"What difference does it make?" said Brad. "It could have been anybody."

"Front door and back door are nailed, as you know," said Piggot. "I studied them afterward. Nails still there."

They walked a few steps down the cobbles, stood in front of the old cheese shop, and gazed at its front.

Its door was shut and empty looking, its single window firmly boarded up with cheap planking.

"What makes a cheese shop different from a lot of other shops?" asked Piggot.

"Cheese," said Brad.

Piggot didn't smile. He said, "It's the cellar. A cheese shop has to have a nice big cellar. With just the right temperature. Well, that's where I found the orange peel, on a table down there. On a table next to a candle stump."

"You weren't going to put your rabbit hutch in a damp, cold cellar, were you?" asked Brad.

"While I was there, I just thought I'd look around a little," said Piggot. "Get off the subject of that rabbit hutch. We're not talking about rabbit hutches, we're talking about this orange peel. Why would anyone go down into a cellar of an empty shop, light a candle, and sit down and eat an orange?"

"Maybe he just had the orange with him and ate it," said Brad, slightly exasperated.

"That's what I think, too," said Piggot. "That he went there to meet someone, say, and had time on his hands, so he just sat down, took out his orange, and ate it."

"But who was he?" said Brad. "And what was he doing there in the first place?"

"Now you've finally got around to it," said Piggot. "I don't know. But I'd surely like to."

"What you don't know won't hurt you," said Brad, aware that the old proverb was utter nonsense.

"I believe just the opposite," said Piggot. "I believe that's what can really mess you up. Maybe we'd better look that place over, you and me. I'll bring a lantern. I mean mighty quick. Tonight. What time?"

"Could be you're right," said Brad impassively. "How about eleven thirty? After Dr. Doddridge is asleep."

It was natural that neither of them gave a thought to Master Duquesne. No one ever gave a flicker of serious thought to the garrulous French candymaker.

At eleven thirty they met on the roof by the chimney and trapdoor to the abandoned cheese shop. Above, the murky clouds choked off all starshine and moonglow. Piggot had shown up with an old crude lantern, a pewter base topped by a squat, open cylinder of paper-thin cow's horn, which gave off about as much light as a fat lightning bug in a brown bottle. Brad said skeptically, "Was that the best you could do?"

"It burns, doesn't it?" said Piggot. "Let's go."

Painstakingly, they descended the ladder to the upper landing. Here, in the small stairwell, darkness stretching down below them, they paused to whisper it over, and form a plan of action. "When you come right down to it," said Brad, "why aren't we at home in bed? What are we here for?"

"That's what we're here to find out," said Piggot ominously.

It was an answer that didn't make much sense to Brad, but he nodded.

"What say we all find out together?" said a coarse, deadly voice behind them.

They turned.

In a sort of thumb-shaped alcove just to the left of the ladder, standing in a jumble of rubbish, was Boston. And it was a pretty vicious-looking Boston, with a glaze to his eyes and a sucking-in at the corners of his mouth that said he was desperate, that his nerves were hair-triggered and all ready to let go.

"Anybody that come in here," he said, "had to come down that ladder. I was waiting."

He had an enormous coachman's pistol in his hand, at full cock, and with a barrel about the size of a boot-leg.

They stared at him, frozen into silence.

Now, in mock humility, he was shaking his head. "So it was you two all along."

"Not us two," said Brad, making a blanket denial.

"Us two what?" asked Piggot.

"Downstairs!" ordered Boston.

"Not us," said Piggot. "We're going back up on the roof. We were headed for the confectionery, and took the wrong trapdoor. We just made a mistake."

"You sure did," said Boston. "Not knowing your own trapdoor. Down!"

The three of them, Boston in the rear, descended to the ground floor. "Now what?" asked Piggot.

"Down!" snarled Boston. "Cellar."

In the cellar, Boston, using the flame from Piggot's feeble lantern, lighted a candle on a long trestle table.

The cellar was arched in brick, with brick but-tresses along its low walls, and floored with slabs of lime-stone. On the tabletop beside the candle stub were a few fragments of orange peel.

"That's the orange peel I was talking about," said Piggot.

"I see it," said Brad, trying to be casual, trying to get off the subject. "Well, these things happen."

"Boston must have left it," said Piggot conversationally.

"Not me," said Boston. "I never seen it until this minute."

When they made no remark to this, he said, "But I must admit it's a joy to behold. If I wasn't sure already, I'd be pretty sure now. I've finally found the right place."

"What place is that?" asked Piggot.

"The place we've been dearly looking for," said Boston, grinning. "The place that might even buy me a little alehouse of my own in England. The place knowed among certain particular parties as far south as South Carolina and as far north as Maine as the cheese shop. The meeting place where the attack on Fort George, and a good many other and even maybe more treasonable acts, was originated and discussed."

"Now that you've found it, what are you going to do?" asked Brad.

"Why, lay in wait, me and a few soldiers, say, and catch these arch-renegades redhanded, and smash it all, them and their goings-on, in one hard blow."

Neither Brad nor Piggot said anything. Their hearts had withered.

"So I was right from the beginning," said Boston with relish. "Hang on to you two whippersnappers, hang on, hang on, and sooner or later you would lead me to my quarry. Which is what you've did. Let's get away from here. Upstairs again; move."

"You don't need us," said Piggot. "You're through with us."

Piggot was scared. And when Piggot was scared, and showed it, the end of the world had come. Now ice went through Brad, ice that was bone-deep.

"What are you going to do with us?" asked Brad.

"How do I know?" said Boston, looking at them as though they were simply figures of vapor. "But one

thing I can tell you. I ain't going to pat you on the head
and turn you loose to upset my applecart."

They started the ascent of the cellar steps, the boys
in the front, Boston doggedly at their heels. Neither
of the boys spoke. Each was badly shaken. Who could
know what was in their captor's mind? They could be
headed for some foul hideaway and leg irons and wrist
shackles, or even worse. They could be headed for a gra-
vel pit, or some scummy lonesome farm pond. You
could be sure this time Boston would take no chances.

At the top of the cellar stairs, on the ground floor,
there was a small square areaway faced on each of
its four sides by a plaster wall and a door; the doors
were open, showing blackness beyond.

Some of these doors would lead into cul-de-sacs, such
as rooms, Brad knew, some into means of egress, such
as passageways. The point was, Which door led where?

Almost intuitively each boy had made up his mind
to break and run. It was now or never.

"Run!" yelled Piggot, heading toward the door
through which they had originally entered, the door
to the upper floors.

Brad started off in a burst of speed. That door had
been his choice, too, but with Piggot's dashing body
in his way, he veered to the left, through the nearest
other opening.

He had scarcely gone three leaps into the darkness
when he tripped over a broom handle and slammed to
the wooden floor.

Almost instantly, Boston's big meaty body slammed
down on top of him, Boston's horny hand circled his
throat from behind, and Boston's hoarse voice said in

a rage, "I should do you in. Right here, where you lay!"

A voice—of all voices in the world, Captain Lynnwood's—said softly, "I wouldn't."

Boston's pressure on Brad relaxed reluctantly, but instantly, and Brad felt himself released. He and Boston stood up.

Captain Lynnwood stood in the doorway, a bull's-eye lantern in his left hand, its powerful beam blinding them momentarily. In his aristocratic blue-veined right hand fist, which seemed at first glance all carnelian seal rings in gold mountings, he was negligently pointing a miniature pocket pistol. "This is a most obedient piece," he said to Boston. "And it has no sense of restraint. Just toss away your weapon, suh."

Boston laid his coachman's pistol carefully on the floor.

There was only one way to describe the Captain as he lounged there straddle-legged, the bronze saber scar gleaming on his thin cheek, an expensive Scottish traveling shawl looped over his shoulders and pinned at one breast with a cameo as big as a pomegranate. He looked lethal.

For the first time since Brad had become acquainted with him, he looked all fighting man, and sinister.

"So it's you I've been looking for," gasped Boston when he was able to speak. "Captain Lynnwood of the Georgia Rangers."

"You know me, I perceive," said the Captain.

"And the seat of the network we've been trying to dissolve is not located in Sumatra Alley after all, but in Georgia!"

Then Boston moved, with almost blinding speed, with the litheness of a viper.

The blade of a heavy sheath knife glowed in his hand, and the hand whipped back for throwing—and Captain Lynnwood shot him.

Shot him at the top of the nose, where the nose bridge joins the browbone, where the entry to the brain is shadow thin.

Boston went to the floor—dead, legs and arms asprawl, mouth agape. Like a big toad, thought Brad.

Captain Lynnwood was recharging his pistol. "The trouble with some of these old-time sailors," he said critically, "is they think a throwing arm is quicker than gunpowder."

"You killed him because you wanted him dead," said Brad. "He had identified you as a rebel and had discovered that the cheese shop was your place of rendezvous. You waited for the knife to show and then shot him. Like you would a quail in Georgia."

"Don't mess around in politics," said Captain Lynnwood paternally. "You've done very well walking a fence line between Empire and Independence and keeping clear of involvement. May I advise you to continue the same cautious course?"

"But I'm a rebel at heart!" exclaimed Brad. "And I haven't been cautious. It just looks that way!"

Captain Lynnwood smiled. "Glad to hear it. I must admit you had me worried."

"Did Piggot get away?" asked Brad.

"Piggot always gets away," said Captain Lynnwood. "I'll swear he's a magician."

"What's going to happen to Boston?" asked Brad.

"If you'll permit me a blind guess," said Captain

Lynnwood, "I'd say that maybe a few patriots will stow him in a cart a little before daybreak, and take him to a lonesome corner of the docks—and start him on his last, solitary trip to sea. I'd like a mug of mulled wine. I wonder if your Dr. Doddridge might have some cloves?"

"Yes," said Brad. "He has."

13

The big oak clock in Dr. Doddridge's chimney corner, that clumsy, irresponsible, overenthusiastic container of misassorted bolts and bent wheels and general dilapidation, which the doctor kept around out of affection and nostalgia, was trying to indicate midnight—though it was nearer to one—by clangs, belchings, whispered asides, and spine-chilling ratcheting. Piggot and Brad, calm again after their adventure, sat on stools at one side of the hearthstone, the doctor and Captain Lynnwood facing them on the other.

Outside, the night silence, wintry, empty, pressed against the fantastically frosted windowpanes, making a little nutshell of firelight and warmth of the workshop. Sumatra Alley, just beyond the foam-frosted doorsill, seemed as far away as Georgia, or even London.

"There was a meeting in the cheese shop called for tonight," said Dr. Doddridge. "If Captain Lynnwood hadn't gotten there early, or, say, if you boys had gotten there a little earlier yourselves, you could well be annihilated by this very moment."

"You mean Captain Lynnwood came all the way from Georgia to attend?" said Brad.

"I couldn't very well take the meeting down there to him," said Dr. Doddridge.

The boys stared at him.

"You mean *you* were the man Boston has been looking for?" said Piggot.

"I'm afraid so," said Dr. Doddridge with a smile.

"Why couldn't you have confided in me!" exclaimed Brad reproachfully."

"It was safer for both of us this way," said the doctor benignly. "You and Piggot are pretty young. A little on the firebrand side, I'd say. No personal offense meant."

"None taken, sir," Brad said thoughtfully. "It's more than possible you're right."

"I thought it was Master Duquesne himself," said Piggot. "That man fools people. He has depth."

"I thought it was Mr. Lundy," said Brad.

They looked at him in surprise.

"Anyone can make a mistake," said Brad stiffly.

"The funny thing," said Dr. Doddridge, "is that I wish he *were* a rebel. We could certainly use him. Loaded with all that courage and honesty."

"Yes," said Brad.

Piggot said, "When Mr. Haney of Philadelphia came to Sumatra Alley that night, he was really headed for you, Dr. Doddridge. Is that right?"

"That is right," said Dr. Doddridge.

"Then why didn't he come directly here?" persisted Piggot. "Why Mr. Lundy's place first?"

"Mr. Haney's mind lives in a world of hounds and hares, scents, cross-scents, and red herrings, if you'll permit a mixed metaphor. We had never met. He always takes precautions."

". . . and survives," said Captain Lynnwood. "And functions. Unhindered, despite his great importance."

"But you, sir," said Piggot to Captain Lynnwood,

"can't be one of us! You are a close friend of the Governor of New York!"

"And he is a close friend of mine, I hope," said Captain Lynnwood. "For I treasure friendships. Yet I am one of you."

To Dr. Doddridge, Brad said, "When you sent me to the King's Arms, with the toothache medicine for Marjoribanks Tapscott, Esquire . . . There was no M. Tapscott, Esquire?"

"But there was Henshaw, wasn't there?" said Dr. Doddridge. "Who is a fervent patriot in communication with a few patriots within the fort itself, and who frequently, when properly approached, has information of interest."

A handful of chestnuts had been pushed into the coals of the fireplace, and now the two boys and their adult companions raked them out and peeled them. The air was filled with the appetizing aroma.

Munching in enjoyment, Dr. Doddridge said, "The really difficult time is ahead."

"But the start has been right," said Captain Lynnwood, with a dreamy glint in his eyes.

"Yes," said Dr. Doddridge.